I0668665

Only a Moment Ago

DEFINED BY LOVE. DENIED BY TIME.

Only a Moment Ago

DEFINED BY LOVE. DENIED BY TIME.

WANITA HUMPHREY

LAGAN
PRESS

an imprint of
THE OGHMA PRESS

OGHMA

C R E A T I V E   M E D I A

Bentonville, Arkansas • Los Angeles, California
www.oghmacreative.com

Copyright © 2021 by Wanita Humphrey

We are a strong supporter of copyright. Copyright represents creativity, diversity, and free speech, and provides the very foundation from which culture is built. We appreciate you buying the authorized edition of this book and for complying with applicable copyright laws by not reproducing, scanning, or distributing any part of it in any form without permission. Thank you for supporting our writers and allowing us to continue publishing their books.

Library of Congress Cataloging-in-Publication Data

Names: Humphrey, Wanita, author.
Title: Only a Moment Ago/Wanita Humphrey |
Description: First Edition. | Bentonville: Lagan, 2021.
Identifiers: LCCN: 2021945009 | ISBN: 978-1-63373-697-9 (hardcover) |
ISBN: 978-1-63373-698-6 (trade paperback) | ISBN: 978-1-63373-699-3 (eBook)
Subjects: | BISAC: FICTION/Romance/Time Travel | FICTION/Women |
FICTION/Romance/General
LC record available at: https://lccn.loc.2021945009

Lagan Press trade paperback edition April, 2022

Jacket & Interior Design by Casey W. Cowan
Editing by Chelsea Carney & Kelly Sohner

This book is a work of fiction. Any references to historical events, real people, or real places are used fictitiously. Other names, characters, places, and events are products of the author's imagination, and any resemblance to actual events or places or person, living or dead, is entirely coincidental.

Published by Lagan Press, an imprint of The Oghma Press, a subsidiary of The Oghma Book Group.

For Glen, Nick, Hannah, Ada and Max

ACKNOWLEDGEMENTS

MANY THANKS GO TO Susette Shreve, my creative retreat buddy; Cindy Freegard, my proofreader extraordinaire; Sarah Kohnle, whose vision for the retreat started this process; and David Woodsmall for his legal assistance when this story seemed to be dead in the water. I'd also like to remember two beautiful Southern Ladies, The Texas Tenors, and Il Divo for the music of romance, Drs. Anz, Trecha, Koreckij, and PTs Kristen Ewers and Tyler Spence for my mobility.

Lastly, I'm thankful for my wonderful editor, Kelly Sohner, and the rest of the staff of Oghma Creative Media for believing and delivering.

CHAPTER 1

YOU CAN RUN, BUT YOU can't hide! The words echoed repeatedly in her head. She had to make them stop, silence them at least for a moment. Concentrate on here and now. She looked around the room. Just as the brochure had promised, the décor was refined. It began in the lobby and continued to the room where the bellman had just deposited her luggage.

The Hotel Gounod was located in the historical center of Saint-Rèmy-de-Provence. The location was a perfect place from which to explore not only the village itself, but also the surrounding countryside. Looking out the street-side window, she found herself facing the Church of St. Martin. A wry smile curled her lips. Perhaps divine providence had guided her here. She opened the window and stretched an arm out into the pleasant afternoon air. How different from the sticky summer heat she had left behind in Booneville, Mississippi. June was always hot in Mississippi, but the summer of 1952 had experienced ten consecutive days of temperatures over one hundred degrees.

Closing the window and turning back into the room, she once again took in her surroundings. If one were going to run away, there could be no better destination than this. Old world charm and ambiance, along with the beauty of the countryside, would surely wash away memories of the other—the place of pain and degradation.

You can run, but you can't hide!

The plane's engines had droned the words during the long flight. In the hired car, tires hummed them on the pavement from the airport in Marseilles to *St. Rèmy*. Now they ran through her head—in the cold tone of his voice—with the dawning of awareness that eventually he would kill her.

She opened the armoire, hung her few dresses on the rod and placed other items into drawers. A wooden case set in the bottom, along with two pairs of shoes, completed her unpacking. Fatigue from the trip took hold so she prepared for bed, but sleep would not come.

You can run, but you can't hide! Well, she had run, but what about hiding? She curled her knees to her chest and wrapped her arms close. A tear, the first she had allowed, slid down her cheek—hiding could only be temporary—she would have to go back.

———————————

ALAIN PHILIDOR WAS MASTER OF all he surveyed. The gardens were resplendent, and joined with a field of lavender and the rolling meadow beyond. They blurred into an impressionist masterpiece, a Renoir perhaps, or a Matisse. One could imagine furled parasols lying in the grass beside ladies ensconced in chairs under the trees.

The old stone house behind him showed the result of the tender care bestowed upon it. Much of the work was his own. With a few days, or sometimes only one day off, if near enough, he came here to lay stones, hammer nails, smooth wood, and create with his hands. And now the house stood, as it must have, well over two hundred years ago. Whether it had been grand or utilitarian, Alain had restored ruins and lands to their former purpose and absolutely refused to remove anything until it proved hopelessly beyond redemption.

A bee lazily inspected blossoms on a honeysuckle vine. He owned the vine so the bee must be his tenant. A quote from Cicero came to mind—something about tenancy and some insect—a mosquito? Or, perhaps not an insect at all—a lizard, maybe. It all had to do with living in the country rather than being a city dweller. The absurdity of his mind's wandering brought a smile—a rare thing of late.

His eyes swept the vista once more then came to rest upon the area he had chosen for the herb garden. It would be small to start—rosemary, thyme, savory, marjoram, and basil. They would season the meats cooked on the outdoor grill in the warm months and flavor stews when the weather turned colder. The savory would be planted specially to make fricot, an Acadian stew he had discovered in Louisiana.

With eyes closed, Alain remembered hot, lazy days and slow, southern nights filled with the scent of jasmine and the sound of bullfrogs. The concerts in the American South had been an agony of stifling heat in outdoor venues, but once freed from the lights of the stage and costumes unsuitable for the climate, there was a world of spicy food to tempt the palate, soulful jazz to make you weep, and a slowness to life that was a brief respite from the toil of the tour.

Reluctant to relinquish the quiet repose of the moment, he reached for the glass holding his iced drink. Condensation had formed moisture on the outside. With his forefinger, he deliberately chased droplets as they skittered down the side of the container. Taking a final pull of the cold liquid, he forced himself from the chair and prepared to begin work. As the spade was thrust into the earth, there was a faint metallic clink. Excited to reveal his find, he knelt down and crumbled clods of dirt to let them sift through his long fingers. This area had been part of the Roman Empire, but there had also been Greeks and Phoenicians here. Gentle rubbing revealed a gold band that was not that old—possibly a woman's wedding ring. The removal of dirt exposed what looked like writing on the inside, but it would need further cleaning to be able to read the inscription. He stuck it into the pocket of his jeans and resumed his task.

Soil tilled and seeds planted, Alain retreated once more to the shade of the lone Holm oak and slouched into an ancient chair. The ice had melted in his drink but the liquid was still cool enough to quench his thirst. Lauren had urged him to buy new outdoor furniture for the location, but the old pieces were still sturdy and had established ownership of the place they occupied. Surveying the afternoon's labor, it was pronounced well done. The herb garden would thrive.

He swiped an arm across his forehead to wipe away the sweat, then stripped off the soaked shirt, mopped his face, and sat back to enjoy the cooling breeze that began about this time most afternoons. He let his eyes drift over the peaceful surroundings and his mind drift as lazily as the wispy clouds in the mostly clear sky. It was safer that way—the not focusing, the not thinking. Those were postponed until a time when the pain could be borne.

THE DESCENDING SUN PROMPTED HIM to finally move. Gathering his shirt and the glass, Alain walked unhurriedly into the house. The kitchen was a large cool room with a beamed ceiling. The stone floor anchored the space with a solid, ageless feeling. Even though being urged to do so, not covering it had been a wise decision. The room was fitted with modern conveniences—microwave, refrigerator-freezer, oven, dishwasher—all hidden within or behind cabinetry that fit the period of the structure. A breakfast table sat in the middle of the room. French doors led to a shaded terrace with a large granite table surrounded by simple hand-made wooden chairs that had been market finds in *St. Rèmy*. Alain placed the glass in the salvaged old European-style sink, then stood for a moment, looked about and nodded approval at the transformation the room had undergone.

He passed through the dining room and entered the living room where a wide stone staircase transected the width of the first floor. On the second floor, he entered the master suite and headed straight to the bathroom. He reached in and turned on the shower, then stripped off the rest of his clothes and placed them in the laundry bin before stepping under the jets of water. It felt good to allow the hot spray begin to wash away the grime of the day's labor.

He closed his eyes and leaned forward with his hands on the wall and willed his jaw to unclench. She was gone and she would not be back—no point in thinking she would. No point in thinking about what was or what might have been. His mind began to clear until there was only the sensation of water coursing over his body—the body that still betrayed him when thoughts of other times in this shower invaded his solitude.

Switching off the water, then slinging a towel low on his hips, Alain started out of the room but remembered the ring. He took the jeans from the bin and retrieved his find. Holding it under water in the sink and scrubbing with a small nailbrush, he removed the last of the dirt. The ring had been made for a small hand. An inscription encircled the inside. Time and Eternity. It slid easily onto his little finger. A tingle ran through his body—no doubt an illusion having slipped a ring that was obviously a wedding band onto his left hand. *Time and Eternity*—what a joke! What a false promise.

He padded through the bedroom and out onto the balcony. Anna had left a bottle of wine chilling and a small plate of fresh, crisp vegetables and goat cheese. How well the middle-aged housekeeper looked after him. Some days it would seem as though she wasn't even in the house had not food magically appeared and clean clothes found hanging in closets or folded in drawers.

The wine and lengthening shadows lulled him. Labors of the day pulled his eyelids downward.

His dream was filled with shadows, voices raised in anger, an arm uplifted, a slender figure falling to the floor weeping. He awoke with a start. The sun had set and a breeze chilled his bare skin. He hurried back into the bedroom, dropped the towel into the hamper, then pulled out fresh underwear, jeans, and a linen shirt. Not bothering with shoes, he walked down the stairs and sat down at the piano.

Prolonged staring at the keys produced the same results as uncountable times before. His muse refused to open the portal to let words or melodies pass. Giving in to defeat, he went out onto the terrace and sat in the gathering darkness.

I sat amid flowers to paint—their colors were glorious, but it was the walls of the city that drew me—perhaps I could draw from them the strength I so desperately needed.

CHAPTER 2

ALAIN LOVED THE EARLY MORNING. Steam rose from the coffee in his mug as he made his way to the old chair in the garden. A light jacket broke the early chill but wouldn't be needed far into the day. Deep breaths brought in crisp air laden with the fresh scents of morning.

Any disquieting thoughts and dreams of the previous evening had disappeared. Coffee finished, he rose, stretched, and set off across the field. His destination was a small copse of plane trees that lay little more than half a kilometer away. Faint barking from that direction led him to believe there might be a den of foxes. Perhaps there would be kits, and the thought of watching them at play piqued his interest.

The grove was at the crest of a small hill, but on approach he stopped abruptly when his attention was distracted by a figure across the nearby meadow. Curious as to who it might be and what they were doing there, Alain stared in that direction. It was a woman sitting on a stool in front of an easel.

There would certainly be a wide choice of vistas to capture on canvas. Beyond the field, perhaps a kilometer or so, lay the village of *St. Rèmy* and beyond that, the foothills of the Alpilles. All attracted artists at one time or another.

He proceeded a few steps then sat on the grass among the flowers to watch.

The woman was young—that was obvious even from this distance. A breeze ruffled her dark wavy hair and the flowing white dress she wore. Her face, visible only in profile, was pale.

The artist placed the palette and brushes on their case and stood up to stretch. She was tall, perhaps almost as tall as Alain. The litheness of her figure was evident in her bending and moving with the grace of a dancer. With no idea as to why he should wish to remain undiscovered, Alain watched and hoped that she would not turn in his direction. Exercises completed, the artist sat once more, brushes and paints were retrieved and work continued.

Alain could see that her subject was the distant village and questioned her choice—most artists would have chosen the fields of flowers.

The history of this area had been an asset when the location for his home was chosen. Encircled by a wall, *St. Rèmy* is a picturesque, active village. Visitors are attracted by a good selection of restaurants and hotels, as well as the lore of historical figures who once resided there.

Nostradamus, known famously around the world as a prophet, was simply known as an outstanding physician in Ancient France. Vincent van Gogh had been voluntarily confined in the Asylum of St. Paul, during which time he painted his Self-Portrait. During World War I, Albert Schweitzer spent time in the hospital here. He was not ill but he was German, which made seclusion prudent.

There were other equally interesting sites within an easy drive. There was Avignon with its palace from the time of the Papal captivity and wild horses on the Camargue. He remembered walking along the top of the *Pont du Gard* as far as was allowed with Lauren calling to him to be careful....

———————

A SMILE BEGAN TO CURL Eudora Winningham's lips. For more than a week she had been alone on the landscape, enjoying the solitude. Today there was a man, who no doubt thought himself undetected, sitting among flowers in the distance. Eudora always knew when a man was watching her. From an early age she had been able to sense when male eyes were following her. Also learned was the fact that when her father thought his observation unnoticed, if her behavior was particularly charming, it earned praise and often lovely presents.

One might think that possessed of this power, a girl would be spoiled, tempted to use it selfishly—but she was not and did not. A gentle soul who truly longed to please, this gift helped her to achieve that goal.

A lifelong resident of Booneville, Mississippi, Eudora was a southern belle by tradition. It is a tradition for which instruction begins at birth with every female relative, no matter how distant, feeling inclined to participate.

A southern belle is not all moonlight and magnolias—that is the façade. Inside there is strength of character, determination, and a will of iron. The same spirit that led women to hide the family silver in the well or stand on the front porch defying the Yankee army during the Civil War is alive and well in the modern version.

Eudora was more than the stereotype suggested. She was a true Southern lady who ordinarily lived by those rules of convention and tradition. Being in *St. Rèmy* had broken those rules.

THE WATCHER SMILED TO HIMSELF. He could not say why observing the painter had given him pleasure, but it had. Perhaps it was that someone obviously appreciated the beauty of this place. He did not care that she had trespassed onto his land.

The artist decided to call it a day. Supplies stowed in the box, stool and easel tied to it, she picked up a bicycle that had lain unseen in the grass. With belongings attached to a strap for transport, a wide-brimmed straw hat retrieved and placed on her head, she pushed her vehicle to a path that led to the village.

Alain watched as the flowing figure became smaller and smaller in the distance. The rider crested a swell in the path then disappeared down the other side, only to reappear as the land rose again. Finally, there was only a small moving dot that disappeared into a thin curtain of air, absorbed against the backdrop of the distant village.

The sun's rays indicated it was after noon. His stomach reminded him that it was past lunchtime and that breakfast had been only coffee. The foxes were forgotten in favor of hunger. The artist was not forgotten—would she return? He hoped to see her again, a thought that for a brief moment registered as odd.

A bowl of fresh fruit waited on the counter and beside it, a plate covered with a napkin that did not prevent an enticing smell from reaching his nose. Anna had made fried chicken, another taste acquired during the tour in the United States. It had become one of his sinful indulgences. Anna did not prepare it often so when she did, every crumb of its crunchy coating was devoured and fingers licked afterward.

A crock of butter from the refrigerator and fresh crusty bread that had been stored away joined a pear on the plate with the chicken. Juggling plate, cutlery, and a beer pulled from the cooler, he carried all safely outside to the old table, then sat to enjoy his repast.

Chicken bones having been picked clean and fingers licked, he sat finishing his beer, then engaged in an hour of idleness of mind and body. Work ethic overcame lassitude. So, determined that the day should not pass without some task accomplished, the reluctant gardener rose and finished weeding a small flower bed and a border along a stone walkway before returning the dishes to the kitchen.

Anna was gone for the day but had left a note telling him that since the sinful chicken had been eaten so late, there was a bowl of salad for dinner and it should have the low-fat dressing. He didn't know if she was that concerned with his food intake or just didn't want him feeling guilty over his consumption of the fried fowl.

His shower was hurried, not long enough for memories to get a foothold, his body to stir, and the pain of loss to set in. He climbed onto the bed, propped the pillows behind his back at the headboard and picked up the reading materials which had been assembled to prepare for restoration of the antique motorcycle that had been his latest purchase.

Though it seemed odd, images of the artist drifted into his mind. Why should a trespassing woman, painting in his field, command so much time in his thoughts? Concentration became more and more difficult until the papers slipped from his fingers as he dozed.

A LONE SPOTLIGHT ILLUMINATED TWO figures on a dark stage. A woman was crying and a man was shouting. She lay on the floor as he loomed above her. The slap echoed in the darkness. Her head snapped back, then drooped as her cries became sobs. The flaming print was visible on her pale cheek before dark hair swung forward and covered it. With feet rooted to the floor, the dreamer could only stand and stare helplessly as another blow rained down upon her.

ALAIN AWOKE WITH A START and felt disorientated until his fingers touched the scattered papers and his eyes focused on the clock on the bedside table. Beside it were his watch and the ring. Its inscription mocked him, *Time and Eternity.* Is it ever true?

Still not fully awake, Alain looked out the window and realized that dusk had given way to night. A feeling of weariness overwhelmed him and dinner was forgotten. He tossed the towel onto the floor, crawled under the duvet, and burrowed his head into the down-filled pillow. He grinned at his decadence—throwing things on the floor and sleeping naked! Evidently the structure of touring or studio recording needed to be reinstated. Oh yes, going back to work was definitely called for.

His night was filled with more sounds of abuse and suffering. The image of a woman with alabaster skin and a cloud of raven hair floated through his nightmares.

Sleep was restless, but the new day brought only warmth and brightness and dreams were forgotten.

EUDORA'S NIGHT HAD BEEN FILLED with horror. The physical abuse from his hand striking her, then the verbal abuse as he hurled accusations at her, were all too vivid and real. And with dawn streaking the sky, her dreams were always too well remembered. Again, the thought ran through her tired brain. *You can run, but you can't hide!* Well, giving it her best effort, she had run. It was the can't hide part that still had to be pushed away into a corner with other dark things. She must clear her mind to think logically and plan her next move. And there must be a next move. She could not escape the fact that she would have to go back, but if she wanted to live, there had to be a plan in place to guarantee her survival. She was not yet ready to begin to formulate that plan. Past and present must first be reconciled.

Dressed and eager to get her day started, Eudora went in search of the little patisserie she had discovered yesterday. The aroma of baking bread reached her before she turned the corner. She purchased a steaming cup of coffee and a bun crammed with raisins and brown sugar, then sat at one of the small sidewalk tables to enjoy her food and the surrounding architectural feast. While pulling feather-light pieces from her pastry, she imagined the pride of the men who had conceived the plans and built this remarkable town. Now considered quaint, it must have been the model of modern wonder at its conception. Had Nostradamus scurried along this very street on his way to see a patient? Would he have sat and pondered the wonders of the universe? Did he work out some sort of equations to arrive at his predictions, or did they come to him in a blinding flash of cosmic revelation? Some research would be in order to learn more about this resident who would later gain such notoriety.

Breakfast finished and curiosity put aside, Eudora prepared to return to her painting. She decided she would *not* return to the same location. The man would be there again, but she must not be. What an odd thought. She turned her steps back toward the hotel.

Begin each new day with new strokes of paint to make your life your masterpiece. Could I possibly make this true?

CHAPTER 3

CRUSHED PLANTS WITNESSED THE EXACT spot where Alain sat yesterday. It was futile to pretend that this had not been his intended destination or that he was not disappointed when she wasn't here. After an hour, defeat was apparent as the light would change and not be suitable for painting the ancient wall. With only wisps of his long hair moving in the wind, he waited. For what? It was already certain that she wasn't coming.

Then for what? Surely, he could not still be waiting for Lauren. She had made it plain that she wouldn't be coming back.

A month ago—or was it only yesterday—or a year ago? Her departure had taken continuity from his life. Their life together had been discussed—planned. He would stay with the group for another four years. During that time, they could have this place refurbished, get married and start a family. By the end of his second contract, there would be enough money, if wisely invested, to ensure that their future would be secure.

Alain planned to resume his solo career on a limited scale and also to teach. Great singers had tutored him, and it was his dream to perhaps do the same for a few talented young students.

Now the place was finished, investments had been made, and his career could carry on. It was the marriage and family elements that had been eliminated. And he had never seen it coming. As a couple, they had begun to spend longer periods of time here and the world had seemed their oyster. But this oyster held only grains of sand, and no pearl of great price had formed within its shell. They sat on the balcony off the bedroom—they had just made love, for heaven's sake. He stared blankly at her, not able to immediately comprehend the meaning of her words.

"Alain, we just don't want the same things anymore." Such a trite statement to produce such unbearable pain.

Didn't want the same things anymore? What things? What had changed? Her eyes weren't cold, they just no longer held the passion that used to burn in them when she talked to him, held him, made love with him. Her words weren't cruel, they simply told of dreams no longer shared, goals no longer held in common. Her voice held the sound of love dying, a death knell for the heart. It tolled for lost faith and shattered trust.

For her, the world travel, trappings of fame, glamorous life they led had become an addiction. To her, this bucolic paradise was a place of exile, never a place to live. It was his idyll.

Had he even made a reply? What would there have been to say? She no longer wanted the life they had planned—no longer wanted him. What he wanted had never entered into the equation—it was decided—it was done— Lauren was gone.

So, work continued here, but he was unable to allow himself to reevaluate because the loss was still too painful. Whatever the future painting of this landscape held, it was certain that he must be in it. Beyond that, a major figure had been painted out which left a void that somehow must be filled on the canvas.

———————

EUDORA PAINTED OVER THE SAME area for a third time. The view wasn't right, the light wasn't right, the perspective wasn't right!

Her instincts had told her to stay away from yesterday's meadow. Although the man had made no move in her direction, there was danger there. Another odd thought because he had respected her space and her privacy, sitting quietly, knees pulled up to his chest with his arms wrapped around them. His proud head was held high and, though unable to be seen from the distance, Eudora was sure that his eyes were gentle and that they had never left her.

Was this land his? Did he farm it? Why did he sit quietly and watch and not come to see what she was doing? Why did her heart beat faster? Why were her cheeks flushed? Why did she know this man possessed a kind heart and gentle nature? Odd that she should make these assessments of him. Her thoughts had become questionable and confusing.

ALAIN WAS NOT READY TO deal with what would come next. Any portrait of his existence would have to remain incomplete for the time being. This was new to his nature—there was always a plan, a vision of how his future was laid out—a blueprint to follow. That had been taken away. There must be time to heal, regroup—time to think logically once more.

Logic had nothing to do with his thoughts of the artist from yesterday. Only seen from a distance, why should there be a feeling of attachment? Observations from the previous day were reviewed. The woman looked tall and slim—with long dark hair—she wore a flowing white dress. White dress? What woman wore a dress into the countryside to paint? There were no answers and each question only created another question.

EUDORA PACKED UP HER SUPPLIES ready to head back into *St. Rèmy*. Today had certainly been wasted. Not one stroke on that canvas was worthwhile, none would be salvaged. But it wasn't as though the masterpiece of the century was going to be created by her hand. Painting was an excuse to be here, something to occupy her time, a reason to stay—away. Going back was inevitable—sometime—not soon—nothing to think about now. Well, she certainly managed to avoid thought of a whole list of things right at the moment. Wouldn't think about....

The case was stowed, and the bicycle turned in the direction of the village—she really intended to go there. But the vehicle seemed to move of its own volition and turned toward yesterday's location and arrived just as he disappeared in the distance. It was the same man.

Though she had not seen him standing yesterday, Eudora knew the man who walked away was he and that her voice wanted to cry out to him to come back. The thought was disconcerting and troubling in its inappropriateness. Something lurked in a corner of her mind—something that could not be recognized or coaxed into the realm of comprehension.

ANNA EMERGED FROM THE PANTRY with her hands full of herbs to add to the pot simmering on the stove.

Startled, Alain jumped, then gave her a smile but not before she noticed that his face had worn a disappointed look.

"I'm sorry, Alain. I didn't mean to frighten you. I was wondering when you would be coming back." Anna Pascale was short, with deep blue eyes and flaxen hair. She was widowed in her mid-fifties when her husband was killed in an accident five years earlier. They had no children, and in answering the ad for a housekeeper here, she had found someone to take to her heart and care for, and Alain had found a friend who kept his home spotlessly clean and running smoothly. She did not pry into his affairs and would never have thought of intruding but was ready to offer him a motherly shoulder or comforting words when the time came that he needed them.

"I was walking over toward the village again. Yesterday there was a woman there painting. I was curious about her and thought I might see her again today, but she wasn't there." The disappointment in his voice caused Anna to look closely at him.

"Well, perhaps another day." She had wept for him when Lauren left. His handsome face was suffused with pain and his gray-green eyes often misted with unshed tears. He was no longer the light-hearted young man who teased then laughed when her cheeks flushed at his remarks. His wicked sense of humor was no longer in evidence and a frown often knitted his brow. He had become leaner and more muscular and had lost any look of softness acquired while touring.

"I see that you finished the chicken yesterday." Her voice held only mock surprise because she had known there would not even be crumbs left.

"You're a bad woman, an enabler. If I end up a fat tenor, it will be your doing." His jovial mood cheered her.

"But you didn't eat your salad." Her admonishment held more than a hint of laughter as she returned to her cooking.

———————

EUDORA STOOD LOOKING ACROSS THE field wondering where the man was going. His home must be nearby. This morning instinct had told her to stay away from this place—she hadn't. Now intuition told her she should not be here—but she was. Her mind said to give up her curiosity about the unknown man—she couldn't.

Questioning her thoughts and actions, she turned and headed back toward the city.

Perhaps terror would not be there in her dreams tonight—but it was. And the demons leapt and blazed around her until one thrust his face against hers and she sat up, sweat pouring from her body, hoping that her unconscious scream had not been given voice.

———————

ALAIN'S OWN SLUMBER WAS NOT peaceful. He tumbled into a void. He spiraled in a whirlpool of darkness. Another figure joined in his endless circling. Trailing wispy white robes and floating black tresses, the phantom partner reached beseeching arms toward him, then drifted away just before fingers could make contact. The ill-fated couple moved up and down within the vortex, never touching.

Escape? How does one escape the terror in the night when leaden feet are unable to move?

CHAPTER 4

THE DREAMER SLOWLY ROSE TO consciousness. There was something—just out of reach. Maybe by lying very still and concentrating, it would take form. Defeat was evident after a few minutes—the world of dreams was gone—wakefulness had banished all hints from his subconscious mind and the elusive memory was irretrievable.

Alain stretched languorously, awakening muscle groups one at a time until his well-toned body was ready to move into action. He thought about the day ahead. He really should call Edward to see if the final dates had been set for going into the studio. Group discussions about content of the album had been long and, at times, heated. In the end, all had been party to give and take and agreed that while the album would be a big risk, nothing like it had ever been done. It would run the gamut of genres—Opera to American country. Once this concept was agreed upon, and it was decided that the risk was worth taking for something so extraordinary, the real challenge began. They were each to do one solo and he had thought about what his should be. His was the voice with the crisp clear quality—the most unique one. He knew he should choose a ballad but could not face the idea of a plaintive love song at the moment.

As genres were chosen, there were long debates as to which of their voices would stand out in a particular area. This let them see where each would have his share of solos, which combinations of voices would work well, and where full-out choruses would be most effective.

The idea of actually going back into the studio sparked the excitement which had been totally lacking lately in his range of emotions. That is, until the day before yesterday—the day a girl in a white dress sat in his meadow to apply paint to canvas.

A quiet calm spread through him as he replayed every minute of his voyeurism. The green of the meadow, scent of the flowers, blue of the sky, caress of the breeze, the perfect scene of a girl with midnight hair, slender arm extended, painting her picture. None of the stress, uncertainty, or heartbreak of his recent life was part of that scene. It was a world yet to be explored. That thought roused him from bed for a shower to remove the last sluggishness of sleep.

Anna was once again in evidence in the kitchen—was that a coincidence? He gave her a quizzical look. Sometimes he felt that her presence was orchestrated—he knew that she worried about him and it gave him comfort to know that she was there ready to listen.

"I thought you might be hungry this morning. Your appetite seems to be better—must be all that garden work you've been doing." Her tone was noncommittal, and her expression gave nothing away. "How about pancakes—the fluffy ones you like with butter and honey?"

Alain stared at her, brows knitted—what was she thinking, what did she want to ask him? He poured a cup of coffee and sat down.

She turned and put her hands on her hips, "Well?"

"Well, I'll have the pancakes, thank you." Then, under his breath, "And I'll have to dig in the garden for two days to work them off." In a matter of minutes, a plate stacked with the pancakes and a glass of juice had joined his coffee on the table and Anna had disappeared to begin her daily chores.

ALAIN USED THE FINAL PIECE of pancake to wipe the last trace of honey and butter from his plate. If left to her own devices, Anna would feed him like this all the time. Evidently, she believed that comfort food might make it easier to solve his problems. He placed dishes in the sink then strode through the door into a sweet-scented breeze and dazzling sunlight.

Garden tools were taken from the shed and work started to even the edge on one of the borders where some rockwork was settling. The task was methodical and tedious, so there was relief as well as satisfaction when it was finished.

He washed his hands in the kitchen sink, drank a glass of water, filled a flask to take with him, and headed once more in the direction of the meadow. She would be there.

The scene below the crest of the rise was complete. Tall grass and flowers swirled and danced in the strong breeze where the artist sat at work.

It was a time about feeling—a sense of calm and beauty simply to be experienced, not thought about, not analyzed—no speculation. He sat—his body quiet—his mind at peace.

The painter painted—stopped and stretched, then painted again. She ate—her motions a study in grace. Delicately pulling pieces from the bread, she finished her food. Her long hair was tossed back so that it floated on the air. And Alain watched.

The spell was broken as he gradually became aware that his breath came in heavy gasps and his thoughts were filled with desire. What the hell was he doing here watching this woman with his body reacting as if he were in one of the Parisian clubs where the women performed in a way to procure such a response? Was the need for a woman then so powerful that it overrode the pain of a failed relationship?

No, it was not the need for some anonymous body to satisfy his physical needs. It was a desire for this particular woman, a woman only observed from a distance, a woman whose face had not been clearly seen, a woman whose touch was only a fantasy, a woman in whose eyes he had not yet drowned.

Disoriented, breaths coming in ragged gulps, Alain pushed himself onto his feet and turned to flee but was compelled to look over his shoulder one last time. Had the sudden movement caught her eye? Had the air actually stirred currents that pushed against her? She stood and turned her gaze full in his direction.

A shiver ran through him. His arm rose of its own accord. The artist waved in response. Alain turned and walked in the opposite direction—and when well out of sight of the woman, he ran.

Ran—winded—crashed through the door—stopped only when he reached the piano. Falling onto the bench, Alain attacked the keys—*fortissimo!* The pain, despair, loneliness, disappointment, fear, and anger all poured out. Composed in his soul, tortured beauty in a minor key was torn from the instrument. Played through numerous times until it was firmly fixed in his memory, he continued to play until the emotion was spent, the feelings acknowledged, then a change of keys, minor to major, a peaceful variation on the previous storm, and words began to take shape in his mind.

EUDORA LOWERED HER ARM IN disappointment. She had gathered her courage to acknowledge his presence and was prepared to walk to meet him and apologize for not having asked his permission to be here. He had turned, looked at her and waved. She had waved back. He had not initiated nor given her the opportunity to move to an introduction but had simply turned and taken his leave.

Surprise and confusion at the man's action dulled her interest in further activity here. Foolish thoughts had been allowed to find fertile ground in which to spring up and grow to a point that there was thought of contact and something more—something unnamed, something deep inside, something primal.

He obviously had no desire to meet her. Her cheeks grew red at the thought she may have made a fool of herself. Ridiculous. Simply a look of acknowledgment in his direction and a return wave could not have betrayed her thoughts. From this distance, he could not possibly have seen what must certainly have been written on her face.

Turmoil reigned in her mind, stealing awareness that the day was still as bright and glorious as it had been only a few moments before.

GRUDGINGLY HER THOUGHTS TURNED TO another day of

glorious sunshine and the air smelling of floral perfume. The day every young woman looks forward to—her wedding day. No detail had been left to chance—no nervous jitters to mar the serenity of the bride.

The plantation gardens were groomed to perfection. The sun shone with gentle warmth, not the scorching heat it would produce in a few short weeks. The clouds were puffy and white. A rain cloud would not have dared to put in an appearance today. It was not the rainbow wedding favored by many modern Southern brides. It was not hoop skirts and broad-brimmed hats. It was understated elegance. It was Eudora.

Briarwood was a favorite location for weddings. Eudora's family would have preferred the church where Campbells had attended for generations, but the young couple had decided on the plantation. Located only two miles from town, it was accessible by horse-drawn carriage, which set the tone for an event in surroundings of a bygone era.

The bride's attendants descended from their carriages and glided down the path in their simple gowns of pale green. The little boy carrying the rings wore an expression that announced how seriously he took his job. The angelic flower girl bent gracefully to pick up a small green leaf—she had petals to scatter and was pretty sure the leaf should have remained in her basket. All joined the groom and his men standing in front of the gathered congregation.

As they walked down the petal-strewn path, Eudora smiled up at the father who had always been her champion and squeezed his arm close to her side. She could see her mother's face beaming from her seat in the front row of organdy-draped chairs. Eudora paused to place a gentle kiss on the cheek of Imogene Ann Westcott Campbell, the quiet, great lady who had loved and guided her to womanhood.

The Campbells were pleased with the match. Joel Winningham was the catch of the county—for that matter, nearby counties as well. And at the end of the path, in front of the arbor covered in ivy and roses, Joel waited for her. The sunlight gilded his blonde hair and a perfect smile was fixed on his perfect face.

They were pronounced man and wife—the perfect wedding, followed by the perfect reception in the plantation house.

The wedding guests departed, the newlyweds ascended the grand staircase to the bridal suite, and the bride retired to the dressing room to prepare for the nuptial bed.

Eudora tied the bow at the top of the filmy negligee. Bridal white, the cut and fabric accentuated her curves and projected a seductive innocence. She sprayed her favorite perfume, cast a final glimpse into the mirror, took a deep breath, then entered the bedroom. Joel was seated on the edge of the high bed but rose as she walked toward him. He raised his arm and Eudora stepped forward expecting to be drawn into a waiting embrace.

The blow knocked her to the floor. Stunned, she could only look up at him with silent tears running down her cheeks and bewilderment in her eyes.

"Don't you ever again come to my bed looking and smelling like a whore!" The angry, vehement words were softly spoken.

She was never to look like a whore, but he used her as one. That night and countless nights thereafter. And when she found no refuge, when the only advice she got was, "Try not to antagonize him," it was self-advice because she was too ashamed and confused to confide in anyone. She knew her parents would support her but was afraid of the direction her father's support might take. She longed to seek the comfort of her mother's understanding arms but knew it would never be kept from her father.

She began to plan her escape.

——————

ALAIN RESTED HIS HANDS ON his thighs. They were done with the keys. Pent up emotions had been vented. Tears ran down his cheeks as his shoulders shook with cleansing sobs.

He started briefly as arms reached around to comfort him and a soothing voice crooned, "Sssh, ssh—it's ok. You cry all you want—tears wash pain from your eyes." A cheek was laid against the top of his head. Anna turned to sit on the bench beside him.

He laid his head against her, and she softly stroked his hair until he was quiet. "Thank you, Anna. I don't know what else to say."

She reached out and wiped a tear from his cheek. "You don't have to say more. I've watched you hurt and knew I was powerless to help. I've been where you are. I know how it felt to have the caring touch of another human being when you hit bottom. I've just prayed that I would be here for you when that time came. I think you will be just fine now."

"Yes, I will," and he meant it.

The disappointment at not finding him in the meadow—the music of the stream calling to me—the beauty of him standing there, waiting—was he aware that he was waiting?

CHAPTER 5

ALAIN HURRIED THROUGH THE FIELD of flowers and gazed toward the ancient walls of the city. She wasn't there! Crestfallen, he turned and wandered aimlessly in the direction of a small stream.

He looked into the rippling current and marveled at the interconnecting pieces of nature's puzzle. This little artery would eventually flow into the mighty system of the Rhone which rises near a glacier in Switzerland. Alternately a torrent, then a large mountain river, it enters France, collects tributaries and flows due south to the Mediterranean Sea. Somewhere in that he felt there was an allegory for man's existence. How tiny, how fleeting is our time here as we are swept along. Why was she not there today?

He closed his eyes, lifted his face and let the breeze skim his features. She was supposed to be there. Her absence foreshadowed the cold mistral winds that the valley would funnel during the winter. Loathe to admit defeat, he lingered until the sun was high in the sky. Having walked back to view a still empty meadow, he had returned to sit immersed in the sound of the gurgling water.

The wondrous workings of nature, which ordinarily fascinated him, brought no solace today. It was incomplete. Realizing that a wallow in misery was close at hand, he heaved a sigh and stared at the stream. The breeze ruffled his hair, the sun warmed his skin, and the water sang to him. Peace infused him and before he stood and turned, he knew that she was here.

She was close enough for him to see the alabaster skin, the fine bone structure, the way her dark hair hung from beneath her hat and cascaded down her back, and her hand raised in greeting.

He waved back and walked in her direction. Walked, when his feet wanted to run.

She approached, extended her hand and with a musical drawl said, "Hello, I'm Eudora Winningham. I'm afraid I have been trespassing on your property for several days now, and I do beg your pardon."

During the tour of the southern United States, he had heard that slow sensual speech pattern, but never as charming as it sounded coming from this woman before him. It held the memory of magnolias in moonlight.

Manners put the proper words into his mouth to introduce himself, assure her that her trespass was forgiven, and issue an invitation to paint there anytime.

"I'm a little out of breath, I'm afraid. I left my things just back there and came over here where I could hear the stream—I guess I've missed the morning sun for painting. Do you mind if I rest here a spell?"

He looked at her with curiosity—not surprised by the accent of her speech, but at the almost quaintness of it. Stretching his hand in a theatrical sweep he said, "Please be seated, ma'am."

She smiled, accepted the hand extended and lowered herself to sit on the grass. Spreading her skirt around her, she created a perimeter of space not to be breached. Fingers fidgeted on the material, then rested lightly in her lap.

He sat beside her, aware of the boundary she had established. Emotions tumbled in his head and rippled across his face. Giving her a sidelong glance, he maintained his silence until blurting the obligatory mundane question, "Are you enjoying your stay in Provence?" It was enough to open the door.

"Very much. I don't think I have ever seen anything more beautiful. I can understand now why artists yearn to work here. The beauty of the flowers and their scents, it's such a heady experience. I had never seen a hyssop plant—those little flowers are so blue. Do you know how rare truly blue flowers are? And such a versatile plant, besides seasoning in cooking, it has many medicinal uses. And the fields of lavender—I absolutely must take some home for sachets." Pausing to take a breath, a blush heated her cheeks. "I have just been rambling on. Mama was always saying, 'Take a breath, Eudora,' and I would realize that I was really running on again." Eyes were lowered and fingers willed to stillness. "Mama also says, 'Don't fidget.'"

"Well, your mama isn't here, and I love to hear you speak." He turned his smile toward her. His breath caught as the eyes that were raised to him were bluer than the extolled hyssop flower. "Eudora," her name had to be said while he still had the power to pronounce it normally—it was threatening to burst from him. Saying her name gave her permanence in his thought. It named the beauty that was hers. It bound him to her.

"Yes, Alain?" His name on her tongue was liquid gold and every part of him was hers from that instant.

"Where are you from, how do you happen to be here, and where are you staying?" He was only too well aware of how her mama would rate that speech. The presence of this woman had turned him into a babbling fool. The situation was surreal—but he was lost in it. The landscape slowly turned around them, a camera taking a panoramic view. Music should waft on the air. On cue, a breeze began and caught tresses as she removed her hat.

Melodic laughter broke the spell, "Well, I'm from Booneville, Mississippi, and I am here on holiday, and I am staying at the charming Hotel Gounod."

"And how did you happen to choose this particular part of Provence?" He held his breath. Surely fate had brought her here. They were destined to meet. All sense of reason had flown. Thought was no longer rational. So, this was what was meant by love at first sight. He waited with bated breath because the sun was hidden behind a cloud when she wasn't speaking.

She laughed. "You will think me silly, but I chose it from the label on a bottle of brandy. I would look at that bottle and I thought the name fascinating. I would dream of visiting that far off place with the beautiful name, the place that produced the Napoleon brandy. When I needed someplace to go in my mind, I came to *St. Rèmy*. Saint-Rèmy-de-Provence."

With the last words, her voice had changed, and a shadow crossed her face. He felt a chill, saw the shadow pass, but did not seek its reason.

The snippet of information was filed away to be pursued later. Something made her unhappy, something that she had needed to flee. No, not just unhappy—afraid.

They discussed their surroundings—to both it seemed a safe topic. She was interested in the landscape, the village, and the history of the region. Alain was in his element. He warmed to his subject and the listener sat fascinated, only occasionally interspersing a comment, or more often, a question. The afternoon sun hanging low in the sky reminded them that hours had escaped notice.

"Well, I'm afraid I must be going if I want to get back to the hotel in time to freshen up before dinner."

He leapt to his feet and offered his hand. She grasped it firmly and stood. Once again, lunch had been forgotten. Had she not brought a lunch today, or been uninterested in something as trivial as eating?

"Have dinner with me," he blurted out. Smiling, lest he had erred, "I mean my housekeeper always leaves enough food for at least two people."

She smiled. "Another time, perhaps?" Laying her hand on his arm, she bade him good day and walked away.

HE DID NOT REMEMBER THE food, only that Anna had not disappointed. The wine she had left chilling heightened his senses. Taking a second bottle and his glass, he drifted into the living room. The piano threw a challenge as his gaze rested upon it. A memory stirred within. A pain—at the point of unbearable—a wind, a zephyr blowing away the pain—a peace—to fill the void—to heal the soul.

His fingers on the keys recreated the music. Words which had begun to take shape now poured from his lips in poignant melody.

Where do I find the wind? Who knows from where it came? It touches and then is gone. Its touch won't come again.

Where do I find the rain? Its drops have ceased to fall. My tears, a poor substitute, will not revive a soul.

Where do I find the sun? Surely as last sparks died, it shattered into pieces.

Within the void that's left, when all hope is lost—a new sun is born.

The winds again will blow, and rains once more will fall, then revived the earth will bloom.

She is the wind, she is the rain, she is that newborn sun.

The glass was drained and refilled. The pencil scratched furiously on the pad, recording the words before they were lost.

The bottle of wine finished, he swayed slightly leaving the bench but steadied himself and then headed up the broad stairs. Humming the tune, the part in major key, he smiled.

His body tortured him until he stripped and entered the shower. At first touch of the sponge, his tension exploded. He breathed deeply as the water washed away the stress from his muscles and mind. It was not the thought of past showers with Lauren that had precipitated his body's reaction. It was the desperate need and desire to know Eudora Winningham of the night sky hair, sloe eyes, and porcelain skin. The desire to press her willowy body to his own, to explore the velvety recesses of her mouth, to take her with tenderness and passion. His body stirred again. Mind and body eventually relaxed, he once more crawled naked under the sheet, feeling its touch and imagining it to be the hands, lips, and body of a sensual Southern woman.

IT HAD BEEN A WHILE since Eudora had evoked such a response from a man. The innocence of his exuberance was endearing. As a single girl, she had marveled at her ability to transform swaggering young men into uncertain boys. It was never intentional—not something she wanted to do and was perplexed when it happened. As a married woman, it was completely inappropriate to notice such a response.

When dating, she was careful of the young men's feelings. She always let them down gently. Therefore, while being disappointed that they were not *the one,* there was a virtual troop of rejected suitors who still held her in great esteem and considered her the epitome of virtuous Southern womanhood. To the men, they felt that Joel Winningham was the luckiest man on the face of the Earth.

Her married status had not kept men from looking. Her unavailability simply made her even more alluring. For the most part, Eudora and the man in question had no awkward moments because he never went beyond *looking,* and the looks were circumspect. The few that were not were met with a return gaze that froze them from her existence.

She did not remember the journey back to the hotel. All thought of dinner had disappeared. She entered her room and once inside the door, turned the lock and immediately began shedding clothing. The trail led to the bath, from which she later emerged, body tingling from the hot water that had not only relaxed tense muscles, but further warmed her already hot skin.

She turned back the covers, lay down and pulled the sheet and quilt over her. She squeezed her eyes tightly shut but could not erase the vision of a muscular body beside her, iron bands to encircle and pull her closer, a face framed with dark curls descending to hers.

Mercifully, she fell asleep, but mercy is not longsuffering. The body that was giving hers so much pleasure turned brutal. The lips that were kissing hers became crushing. The strong arms holding her became a prison and when they released her, it was only to move far enough to raise then strike the first blow....

ALAIN TOSSED UNTIL THE BED resembled a battleground. Sheets entangled him so that he could not reach the woman suffering abuse. She was being beaten, but he could not come to her aid. The abuser's back was to him yet there was a familiarity about the figure. If only he could see the face....

I cannot find the words to speak of my first contact with Alain Philidor on that beautiful day in 1952. All was revealed so slowly—the peacefulness of the place to sit and paint—the perfection of the day—the man sitting stoically watching—the first meeting.

CHAPTER 6

MORPHEUS TOOK THE VISIONS WITH him, and Alain awoke with no memory of the confusing dreams. His quick shower was just a shower, then after dressing in haste, he bounded down the stairs.

He grinned when Anna gave a gasp of surprise as he swooped into the kitchen and whisked her into the air. Singing "Good morning!" in a lilting voice, he proceeded to swing her a full circle before setting her feet back on the floor.

She put her hands on her hips and burst out laughing. "Well, what has improved your spirit?"

"Madam, you whip up some of those pancakes while I pour coffee and juice, then join me and I will tell you a tale." His inner child was loose—young, free, and uninjured. "I know, I'm sounding like a complete idiot, but Anna, it's all gone. All the hurt, the injured pride, the feeling of inadequacy—all of it." Again, song burst forth, this time to the tune of "Maria" from *West Side Story.* "Eudora, I just met a girl named Eudora...."

Anna sidestepped his attempt to grab her again, joined the contagious laughter, and plated the cakes which had already been cooking before his dramatic entrance. She sat down and he plopped onto an adjacent chair. Catching both her hands in his he said, "Thank you again for seeing me through this."

"You know I'm glad that I was here. But Alain, this is all so sudden—

you're sure you're not jumping into something too quickly?" Concern crept back into her voice.

He took a deep breath, "I know, I was indulging in a bit of serendipity, but Anna, it is such a relief to actually feel good again. I won't jump into the deep end of the pool, nor will I soar so high that I become as Icarus, fated to plummet to an ignominious end."

As they ate, he related the details of meeting this Paragon of Southern Virtue. His eyes clouded. "She's married, Anna. She wears a ring." A simple statement. "But I know something isn't right. I heard it in her voice."

"Just be careful and proceed slowly." He saw the concern that filled her eyes as she spoke.

"I promise that I am in complete control of my faculties. It's just that yesterday was so intoxicating, and it wasn't because of the two bottles of wine I finished off last night."

She raised one eyebrow and looked at him. "And here I was thinking I must have miscounted how many bottles I chilled. No wonder you're giddy this morning." This accompanied by a grin.

"My feet are on the ground, but I can tell you there is something—something I can't explain—and I'm happy. For the first time in weeks, I felt real joy. Joy just to talk to her." The lines of sorrow were gone from his face. "Anna, could you put together a little lunch? I just have the feeling that I will see her again and we can sit and talk and have some of your wonderful food. I'll use your fantastic culinary skills as a ploy to get her to come to dinner!" He laughed.

"Give me fifteen minutes and it will be ready."

"I'll be back in then," he called over his shoulder as he stepped out the door into the garden. He whistled while filling the bird feeders. Even though it was summer, and nature provided a bounty, he supplemented it. So, who cared if they were a flock of freeloaders—no, never that, their singing more than paid their bill.

Anna came to the door and handed him the backpack. "Enjoy your day. There will be enough for two for dinner if you can snare a guest!" Her laughter followed him as his feet began their familiar trek.

EUDORA LAY VERY STILL. IF she moved too quickly, the pieces might not have time to collect themselves. These dreams, these nightmares, these remnants of waking reality left her shattered and only by lying quietly and giving the broken bits time to reassemble into at least a facsimile of a real person could she hope to rise and face another day. But today shards did not have to be retrieved from so many dark or hidden places. There was an illumination that made it easier to locate them and cement them and breathe life into them so that the cracks hardly showed.

Dressed with care, hair brushed until it shone then tied loosely with a red ribbon, more mascara than usual and cheeks touched with a bit of rouge, she stared at the woman in the mirror, the woman who looked back at her with a happy smile and wonder in the deep reflecting pools of her eyes.

She touched fingers to her lips. How long would it be before he touched them? He would, of course. A shake of her head flung away a dark thought that had crept near. Joel had run his fingertips over her lips, telling her how lush they were, then punishing them with his kisses. Sometimes her teeth had cut the insides of them, but she had dared not cry with the pain. His pleasure in tasting the blood was obvious as his tongue sought to inspect what was savagely torn.

She picked up her hat and case, hurried past M. Jacques in the lobby with a quick, "Good morning," and was on her way. Spirit soaring, feet flying on pedals, hair streaming behind her, she raced toward the rendezvous point. Before cresting the hill that would bring her onto the edge of the meadow, she slowed, lowered her feet to the ground and paused until her breathing had returned to normal.

He was there. Of course, he was. She rode leisurely to within a few inches of him and stopped. He took hold of the handlebars, and when she had dismounted, laid the bicycle on the ground. Then taking both of her hands in his said, "I was afraid you wouldn't come." That wasn't the truth, of course.

Raising her lashes, she looked directly into his eyes and smiled. "You, sir, are a terrible liar."

"Yes, I am!" Both laughed heartily but then were suddenly shy as they became conscious of still holding hands.

Alain broke the spell of the moment by shuffling around to pick up the hastily dropped backpack. He pulled out a small blanket and spread it on the ground. "M'lady, I have a better seat to offer you today." He busied himself with the contents of the pack. Her trembling hands accepted the cup of water poured from a flask. She had kept them relatively calm, arranging her skirt, today closely tucked under her legs, not spread out as a warning sign.

His voice eventually broke the silence. "I want to know everything about you…." a look of distress crossed his face, "…I mean…." his voice trailed off as her eyes raised to look straight into his.

Conflicting emotions struggled across her features. Honesty won the battle and with a deep sigh her course was set. "I am Eudora Eugenie Campbell Winningham. As I told you, I am from Booneville, Mississippi. I am an only child. I am married. I have come to Saint-Rèmy-de-Provence to escape." She tucked her chin.

His eyebrows rose quizzically. He was quiet.

She raised her face. Fire glinted in her eyes. "I have come to Saint-Rèmy-de-Provence to escape because my husband beats me, and it is not my fault. I do not deserve it, and I will no longer stand for it!" It was said. The words could not be unsaid, and she would not wish them to be. They were liberating, they were shared, and she would never again be alone with their torment.

She was quivering, in need of comfort, but he did not touch her—at least not with his hands. Yet his eyes caressed and soothed and in their depths was the man who was all that she wished her husband to be. Sensibility whispered that she did not know this man well enough to know that. She told sensibility to, "Shut up!" This was a kind and gentle man and that was all that this moment required. "What about you?" Her voice whispered and her look implored, "Show me your soul."

———————————

"I AM A RECLUSE HERE because the woman I planned to spend my life with left me, and I thought life could not go on without her. It was not my fault, and I didn't deserve it, and I refuse to continue feeling inadequate because of it." His trembling mirrored hers. It was enough for now.

WITH THESE AFFIRMATIONS, DOORS SPRANG open and light flooded into dark corners.

Tortured with guilt that she should have known what Joel was, should have recognized some signs, had burdened her with misplaced blame. Alain felt that he should have perceived that the relationship with Lauren was failing and been able to prevent it. In this liberating moment, both accepted that they were blameless and forgave themselves for the anguish they had allowed to color their views. Truth and honesty had tumbled forth, and for several minutes they sat breathless, stunned then relieved at what had been shared. The words had flowed of their own accord, and the lips from which they had sprung slowly lifted at the corners, and shy smiles lit up their features.

Attention returned to their surroundings. The backpack yielded bread with a paper-thin crust and feathery interior, a delicate, creamy cheese, fresh peaches, and two bottles of his favorite Grenache. "I think the only things Anna forgot were the candles and romantic music," he laughed.

"The food will suffice. I'm suddenly starved." She accepted the wine he had poured for her. "Do you own this beautiful land? Is this how you make your living? Are you a farmer, a wine producer?" Small talk was becoming much easier.

"Actually, I'm a singer—our group is called Four Point O."

This was met with a questioning look.

Obviously, there was no name recognition here. "I'm not surprised that you've never heard of our group," he chuckled. "We do what is called crossover music. We are all classically trained singers, but most of the songs we sing are popular, romantic songs. Some are sung in English, but many are done in Spanish or even a few in French."

"Now I feel a little embarrassed. I should have heard of you. So, where do you perform, how many of you are there, how long have you been singing? Okay, Mama, I'm taking that breath now…." She laughed and he joined her.

He told her the story of four young music students who had met at a music festival in Austria while they were still in high school. Somehow the three tenors and a lone baritone had gravitated to each other. They quickly found their harmonies meshed into something pretty amazing. They were serious about classical music, but they were also young. Rock was where it was happening, so rock is what they sang.

They were a virtual United Nations. Alain was from France, Aldo from Italy, Antonio from Portugal, and Greg was from the United States. When one of them mentioned that it was too bad that his name didn't begin with an A also, he laughed and said it was their lucky day—his middle name was Aaron—the fourth name beginning with the letter *A*.

He told them that under his country's educational grading system, together they made a perfect grade point average. The others decided that it was a catchy idea, and perhaps one day they would be huge stars in the United States! Youth was the time for such dreams. They quickly became Four Point O. The playbills read 4.0 and caught on.

They cut a record that met with mild success, then toured small clubs in Europe for two summers. They reached a crossroads and rather than commit to a music career in this genre, they went their separate ways and continued their studies.

Then came crossover! It was made for them—or they were made for it. They considered it another sign that they had started reaching out and reconnecting with each other simultaneously. Four albums and two world tours later, they were still not widely known. Their brand of music received scant airplay, yet they sold out huge arenas on their concert tours. The romantic songs had garnered them a large following.

They were rich, but not beyond their wildest dreams—though that was on its way. They were still down-to-earth friendly men and their fans adored them. They were taking a well-deserved rest, then beginning work on their biggest album risk so far and planning the next tour.

"We have been incredibly fortunate," he concluded modestly.

"And I repeat, I can't believe that I haven't heard your music."

"You can hear it. I will play it for you. Come home with me." His words were quiet, earnest, but also left no doubt that it was more than a simple invitation and would encompass more—so much more.

Her response indicated that she was not offended by what was in his voice. Moistened lips carefully framed her words. "With all my heart I wish that I could, but I cannot. Please understand."

"I do." They quietly packed the remains of their lunch, then stood. His embrace was gentle and fleeting, "I'll be back."

"As will I," was the quiet reply.

He stood motionless and watched until once again the bicycle melted into the ancient walls of the city.

I did not accept his offer of dinner at his home—that was for another day—I knew there must be another day. I would not think of the implications of that.

In retrospect it should seem odd that we shared our deepest hurts during such an early meeting—but it does not seem odd now, nor did it in that moment. It was as natural as a Sunday afternoon conversation between old friends.

CHAPTER 7

ALAIN CARRIED THE TRAY HOLDING fresh greens, crusty bread, and a steaming bowl of Anna's special mushroom soup to his favorite spot. A deliberate man, he savored the subtle flavors of the soup and the spicy herbs that had been added to the salad.

Eating outside, letting the ever-changing landscape paint pictures into his mind and a gentle breeze bring the perfume of blooming things to seep into his skin, was the perfect finish to this day. He sat a while longer, reluctant to leave the tranquility of his surroundings. Provence had a scent, a look, a feel that made him desire the simple life and renewed him when his life was less than simple.

The failure of the relationship with Lauren was not his. It had not been in his power to prevent its inevitable doom. She had changed but matching her change would have meant losing the very essence of himself. That did not, however, ease the pain of lost love. Alain had truly loved her but realized that the seemingly trite platitude, *sometimes love is not enough,* was actually true. It was the trying to hold on that had given him such pain—pain that had now been left on the grassy bank of a bubbling stream.

The fact that he was falling in love—no, *had* fallen in love—with a married woman would require greater deliberation. For an honorable man to covet a woman who was bound to another was against everything in his nature. But covet her he did—desired her with his heart, and wanted her with his body.

There would be thoughts of her with great tenderness and purity, but then the fire would grow deep inside and there would be the need to know her, to *have* her.

He pushed the tray from him then rested his head on folded arms. The breeze sent strands of hair playing over his cheek and imagination made it hers as she leaned over him, her hands running down his arms, her body pressing against his back—she would whisper in his ear—he would stand, turn and pull her to him....

———————

EUDORA DID NOT RIDE WITH the energy exerted on the earlier trip. Her legs felt reluctant as they were forced to turn the pedals. Each circle of motion took her farther from him. He had asked her to come home with him. Home. That was not the house where she lived with the man who was her husband. Not yet having seen Alain's home, she knew that was where her life belonged—because he was there. Because when she thought, "I must go home," that meant, "I must go to where he is."

That knowledge was in her heart. Riding farther from the place where they had sat together, her head began to regain control. Was it possible? Could the old life be left behind and a new one made here? He loved her. Whatever mystical spell had encapsulated them, had imbued them with the certainty that they each loved the other. Each knew it and sensed rightly that the other also knew. It was clear that there were only two choices. She could return to the old life or go forward to the new. She was obligated to one but desired the other with all her heart.

———————

ALAIN RAISED HIS HEAD, THEN his arms, and stretched. Muscles that were beginning to cramp told him that he had sat in the same position for quite some time. He leaned his head back, closed his eyes, and rolled his shoulders until relaxation began. He straightened and ran an assessing gaze around the garden.

Climbing roses by the wall caught his eye. Their care had been neglected. After carrying the tray into the house, he walked to the garden shed where he picked up clippers and a basket, then proceeded to deadhead the roses. A few leaves needed to be pruned, and some branches should be anchored until they grew in the proper direction. The garden benefited from an hour of clipping here, arranging there. The location of a flower or perfection of its blossom often prompted a leisurely pause in appreciation. He disposed of the clippings, returned the tools to the shed, then strode into the house.

A hot shower revived him. Alain pulled on clothing then descended the stairs and surveyed his surroundings. It was a comfortable home. Home. It was a house where he lived. It would be a home when she resided here with him.

Anna would be wondering about her wine count again. Two bottles and a glass were on the tray placed atop the piano. With candles added, the musician was ready to begin.

Tension flowed from his body as music flowed from his fingertips. The songs were songs of love. Quiet ballads, peaceful and full of tenderness. Pictures reeled through his mind. Every word, every glance, every gesture of hers was relived in the melodies.

He replaced the second bottle of wine in the cooler, made sure the candles were extinguished, then climbed the stairs and entered his room. The large bed before him no longer looked a wasteland, but a land of promise. She would share it. A smile curled his lips, "Eudora," he sighed later as sleep crept in.

THE DEMONS THAT INVADED THEIR sleep flitted from one to the other. In his, they were vague and faceless but in hers, they were all too recognizable. They screamed in their minds and burned in their bodies.

Leaving her to a moment of peaceful slumber, they stormed through his night giving him no rest. Tossing fitfully, then awakening startled, his recollection of the dream was excruciatingly accurate. Escaping from the knotted sheets, the dreamer fled onto the balcony. Staring into the starry sky brought no calm to his troubled spirit. Leaning on the railing, eyes closed, realization flowed over him. The dreams had started just before first seeing her. He remembered that now. Was this an insight to the nightmare that was her marriage before she had ever told him of the hell in which she lived? Had there been a connection, knowledge before words were ever spoken between them?

"Eudora," he whispered into the stillness. "What am I going to do about you?" The query was there for him to answer. "I am going to love you forever." His reply settled the future. They would be together.

Returning to the bed, he straightened the sheet enough to pull over himself and dropped into undisturbed slumber.

THE FIENDS CIRCLED HER, DANCING in demonic delight. She was dizzy from turning in circles, watching for the next to advance to prod her with sharp instruments. Pain and despair enveloped her. Even in slumber, hopeless tears flowed down her cheeks as she descended into the abyss. Long legs strode through the fiery ring surrounding her. Strong arms pulled her close to a muscular body. Tender hands stroked her hair and urged her tortured head to rest against a broad chest. They stood thus, in quietness, all else banished. "Alain," she whispered as she awoke. "Alain," she whispered as she entered sleep where she was the only inhabitant.

So, the tug of war begins—mind's sensibility—heart's desire—home—home?

CHAPTER 8

JOEL WINNINGHAM DROVE THIRTY MILES an hour above the speed limit as he hurtled through the night toward Booneville. Trips to Jackson always exhilarated him and spurred him to reckless behavior. This trip had cost him a pretty penny, and it was his bitch of a wife who was to blame. He had taken his rage out on the woman of the evening, making it necessary to pay enough extra to take care of her until she was able to work again.

Now he sped through the night, top down, hair blowing in the wind and silvered by moonlight.

He would have to frequent a different house now, of course. Angelique would not report him to the police for what he had done to one of her girls, but she would never allow him in her house again. Pity—she had the prettiest and most talented girls in the state. Of course, there were always neighboring states. That might be necessary as word could get around the houses in Jackson and even further and he would find it difficult to gain admittance to the class of establishment he required. There would never be any public scandal and no gossip passed that would tarnish his reputation, but in silence he would be denied what he sought.

He thought of his wife. Beautiful, perfect Eudora. Before their marriage he had given much attention to being the perfect suitor. She had heard no gossip—actually because there wasn't any. He had been very careful—there was the Winningham name to uphold—the place in society—the reputation needed for business. Choice of establishments and some long-term liaisons had kept his debauched life private. He wondered for a moment if he was growing careless.

As the wedding approached there was the question of what to do about Eudora. Should he wear the mask of the perfect husband and fulfill his darker needs in the usual way? Yet the idea of her, compliant to his demands, totally at his mercy—these were thoughts that had proved to be beyond resistance. A true sociopath, he was delusional about his ability to control his behavior.

He had been careful not to do serious injury or leave marks that would show, and he always exhibited just enough contrition to convince her that it would never happen again. Of course, it did, but infrequently enough that he could make her believe that staying was better than the humiliation of divorce.

Early on he had wondered briefly if she had said anything to her parents about the situation. Not her mother, because that lady would never have let her daughter stay with him. She would have quietly removed Eudora from his reach. "And not her father, because here I am still alive!" His laughter at this died away as the reality of that possibility sobered him.

He had been smug, so he was completely taken by surprise when he found her missing. His explanation to those who inquired was that she had gone to a spa to "take the waters." He assured her parents that she had insisted that she needed some time alone, then he made sure he avoided them. He considered hiring a detective to look for her but decided that it wasn't worth the money, confident that she would have no choice but to return, and soon.

"You had better get back here, Eudora," he shouted into the darkness. "You had better get back here," growled through clenched teeth. There was no light, no sanity in his eyes as he watched the road in the beam of the headlights.

———————

ALAIN HAD BEGUN TO REMEMBER and dread his dreams. He was bewildered as to why they should haunt his sleep—no, actually, why they should even exist. Was it latent anger about Lauren? It couldn't be. Night after night the woman in his dreams was abused. And that woman was definitely

Eudora. The man always had his back to the dreamer, but he was slowly turning his face into view.

———————

THE DAY WAS OVERCAST—IT matched his mood. The dreams were taking their toll. They were occupying too much time in his thoughts. Why were they occurring in the first place? Why were there visions of Eudora being beaten even before he was aware that it was a picture of reality? Who was the man in the dream—logically her husband, but there seemed to be further significance. What did it mean? Was there someone other than her husband?

The crisp breeze rustled the leaves of the oak and penetrated the light jacket he wore. The coffee carried out with him had cooled quickly. The sky was becoming heavy and if it rained, there would be no artist painting in his meadow—no fascinating woman waiting by the stream.

He considered driving into the village to see her. The idea was immediately discarded—if she felt he was pushing too hard it could spoil everything. He thought of phoning but brushed that aside with much the same reasoning.

As the first drops began to fall, he picked up his cup and hurried inside. There were several small projects awaiting his attention, but there was no point in even trying to choose one knowing there would be no concentration while his mind was occupied with his need to know more about this woman.

———————

EUDORA STARED AT THE STEADY stream cascading down the windowpane. Knowing that there would be no going out today, she had taken her time about getting dressed. Sitting near the window in an ivory robe, she was an old photograph in black and white. Melancholy passed as she began collecting and processing random thoughts into a cohesive plan. Plan. There it was—the word had been thought, if not uttered aloud. A plan was necessary and until this moment it had not been within her power to even lay the foundation for one. Now there was a foundation—Alain Philidor.

For the first time in her life, Eudora knew what it meant to fall in love. Love with Joel had been a young love, first blush, romantic fantasy—what a fool she had been. Why had deception been so easy? No going down that path of self-blame ever again! She had been young, innocent and trusting. Her youth and innocence had been stolen and her trust shattered. Evil existed—it lived in her home—slept in her bed—it had controlled her life. But no more.

Alain Philidor. He was a musician, obviously a reasonably successful one. While his hurt had not been physical, he had been emotionally devastated. She still found it remarkable that they had both just burst forth with their private hurts while relative strangers. And yet it had seemed so natural, as though they were not strangers at all.

A plan. Then she knew—the plan would be to simply embrace the joy that would come and at some point, walk willingly into the arms of a handsome young Frenchman. Although an oversimplification, it was a start and all that she was capable of at the moment. It was more than she had only a moment ago.

Dressing, tidying the room—all done with slow deliberation. Her mind was finding words—forming sentences, experiencing new emotions—sending smiles of joy to her face. Settled again in the chair near the window, she picked up her journal and began to write once more.

I stepped through the garden gate...

CHAPTER 9

EUDORA WOKE AS SUNLIGHT STOLE past the edge of the window blind and fell across her face. She rolled onto her side, thereby eluding the offending shaft of light, before opening her eyes. Waking gently—waking gently? Muscles moved involuntarily and snapped her to an upright position. She had fallen asleep early the previous evening and now it was bright daylight. A glance at the clock told her that she had slept a full nine hours. Nine hours! No nightmare! When was the last time her sleep had not been interrupted by relentless returning terror? Disbelief gave way to gratitude as her head bowed in silent prayer.

She lay back, pulled the sheet over her shoulders, turned her face into the pillow, and wept. Not the terrified wracking sobs that had so often begun her day, but a soft flow of tears. Tears washing away the old. When they were done—when quiet was restored—when life began again—she made quick work of preparations for the day.

ALAIN WAS NOT AS FORTUNATE. The dream was there, the abuse horrifying. His inability to prevent it was sickening. He tossed, turned, dozed, and finally screamed, "What the hell?"

Leaping from the bed, he staggered out onto the balcony where he sat until a few hours before dawn. Exhausted, he fell back onto the bed and slept for a brief time.

When he awoke, food and work were given no thought as he set off.

She wasn't there. Had too much transpired, did she regret the things said? Should he have tried to contact her yesterday? His thoughts whirled, his movements jerky and frenetic. Doubts nagged as relentlessly as the nightmares. Maybe by the stream. Quick steps covered the distance but at first look were not rewarded.

As he turned back, she emerged from the trees.

THE RAIN OF THE PREVIOUS day had freshened the landscape. Sunlight made diamonds of the few drops that still clung to leaves and branches. The breeze still held the freshness that it retains after a shower.

He was not there among the flowers. Her heart gave a quick flutter but there was not crushing doubt. Beyond the stand of trees, near the stream, that is where he would be. He turned as she came into view.

"Had you given up on me?" Her question was rhetorical.

"Never." His whole face beamed. An answer was not needed or even expected, but never would an opportunity be missed to let her know by word or deed that her every query, every comment, would be considered worthy of acknowledgement.

Their eyes drank deeply before thoughts stirred them to action. They sat on a nearby outcrop staring at the gurgling water. Where words had poured from them at their last meeting, today they seemed to be hiding lest they should be the wrong ones, ones that could damage the fragile beginning that must be nurtured at all cost.

"I was considerably behind schedule this morning because I overslept." Her voice was tentative. "Alain, when I told you about my husband and what I have endured, I did not tell you of the horrible nightmares that I have. Every blow, every insult, I live over and over in my dreams. I wake screaming and terrified. Sometimes the dreams are almost worse than the attacks themselves."

He reached out and placed his hand on hers, curled his fingers around it and enclosed it in a grasp of comfort.

"I am so sorry...."

"No." Her interruption took him by surprise. "You don't understand. I overslept this morning because I did not have those nightmares last night. I can't remember the last time I was free of them. Don't you see—it's because of you." She dropped her gaze and blushed. "I mean, being able to tell you about it—having someone to share my secret with, someone who would share in return—okay, Mama, being quiet now." Her laugh was light, and the face raised to him was open and without fear.

"Are you ready to see my house now? Just see my house—my gardens. I think we have appreciated our surroundings here adequately." His laughter was also light, and the invitation held no hidden expectations.

"I was afraid you might never ask me again." This laugh was teasing.

After being helped to her feet, her hand remained loosely tucked into his as they walked back to where she had left her belongings. Her transportation retrieved, he pushed the bicycle to the nearby lane. They walked quietly until he veered onto a smaller path.

"Am I being abducted into the deep woods?" Feigned fright.

"Actually, this path leads right up to the back gate of my garden." He twirled an imaginary mustache. Both grinned at the light-hearted banter.

Eudora stepped through the rustic wooden gate that was pushed open for her. He stepped to her side to observe her reaction to the garden.

"I can't remember the last time I saw anything this wonderful," the words were barely breathed, "we have beautiful gardens at home, but nothing like the perfection of this. This is Eden." She followed him as he took a stone pathway that led to the kitchen door. For the first time, the charm and beauty of the cottage attracted her attention. She reached out and laid her hand against the ancient stone.

He leaned the bicycle against the wall. "Sorry to be taking you in through the back door, but this is the most convenient entrance from the garden." Again, his gaze held contentment as he watched her reaction to his home.

SHE WAS IN A FAIRYTALE—a beautiful garden, now an enchanted cottage. Having passed through the kitchen and dining room, she found herself in a living area that was roomy and comfortable with a wall of French doors leading out into a side garden. Alain pointed out that a television and music center were hidden away as conveniences in the kitchen had been. The room was filled with comfortable chairs and settees accompanied by side tables and lighting. A piano stood in front of the windows. Here the stone floor was scattered with small rugs. The rich browns, muted lavenders, and moss greens extended the colors from outside the house to its interior. Windows were left uncovered so that the vistas beyond joined the design inside. It was a room with books and personal mementos. It was a room for being with friends, for conversation, for music, for sharing.

"I cannot find the words to describe this exquisite place. It is so beautiful—so perfect. Why would anyone ever want to leave here?" Looking at his face quickly to see if she had misspoken, stirred memory of old hurt, but his face showed only pleasure at her words.

"You see it as I see it, thank you. Now, Anna has gone into the village as it is her shopping day. I am sure there has been enough food left to feed an army for lunch. Shall we dine in the garden? If you would care to freshen up, there is a powder room just opposite the staircase."

The room was tiny but had the necessary convenience and an antique wash basin. She caught her reflection in the mirror and paused to look more closely. Who was this woman in the mirror who looked back at her with such composure and, yes, even joy? It was the woman she had been before the evil that was Joel Winningham had entered her life. The woman she was before her innocence and dignity had been stripped from her. The woman who once again saw the world as beautiful and full of promise. She splashed water on her face and patted it dry with a colorful guest towel selected from the basket on a shelf by the wash basin.

Alain had been busy in the kitchen. A large tray laden with fruit, fresh vegetables, cheese, ham, a loaf of bread, and some little covered pots, was already on the counter. Eudora took the bottle of wine and two glasses he held toward her. He added napkins and cutlery to the tray then headed toward the door. She stepped in front of him, tucked the bottle of wine under her arm, leaving a hand free to open the door for him to pass.

They shared directly from the tray. Pieces of fresh produce were exclaimed over and savored. The little pots yielded fresh butter, jam, and a creamy herb dip for vegetables.

Alain smiled as Eudora made a soft humming sound as she licked a smear of jam from her forefinger. Catching his eye, she chuckled. "You must think I was never taught any table manners."

"I am quite sure you could hold your own with table protocol anywhere."

He insisted she remain seated while he carried the remnants of their lunch inside. Appetites satiated, they sat lazily enjoying the remainder of the wine and watching a few butterflies that had come to drink from the flowers.

"I really should be heading back." Loathe to break the spell of silence but realization that the afternoon shadows had grown long, prodded both to motion.

"Could I drive you? We could put the bicycle in my car."

"Actually, I need the exercise after all of that wonderful food."

"But it was all good, healthy things." His lips curved into a smile. "Well, maybe not the butter and jam."

"And I think we finished every bit of those. It was wonderful. Thank you. It has been a long time since I have felt so relaxed and unburdened."

The silence was becoming awkward. "Could I show you some of the country-side around here tomorrow? There are some historical sites and other attractions. I could pick you up at your hotel about nine."

"That would be lovely. I'll meet you in front of the hotel at nine." Later she remembered that he had visibly been holding his breath. She also remembered that she had responded quickly.

———————

HE HELD THE BICYCLE FOR her, then watched as she pedaled away.

It occurred to him that riding the distance which could easily total almost three kilometers, did not seem to faze her at all—something to ask her about another day.

A small smile turned up the corners of his mouth. His work had all been worth it. This woman recognized that what he had achieved was a setting to be lived in, to be enjoyed, to be valued. He had watched with pleasure as she had studied details in the garden and inside the cottage itself. A comfort had settled in—his house had found approval and in return had granted acceptance.

Do knights always ride in on white chargers?

CHAPTER *10*

"YOU HAVE GOT TO BE kidding!" Her mouth dropped open in surprise. What began as a chuckle morphed into a full-blown laugh.

His Cheshire cat grin told her that he had meant to astound. She did have to admit that he cut a dashing figure sitting on the huge motorcycle.

She was wearing her flat-soled shoes but was wishing that she had been more thoughtful when throwing things into her suitcase and had packed some slacks. A doubtful look met his beckoning for her to join him. He dismounted and reached for her hand as Eudora stepped forward with more than a little trepidation.

"Had I envisioned a motorcycle trip, I would have packed differently." Her voice and look still held skepticism.

"You'll be fine." He straddled the bike then took her hand to help her mount behind him. "Just tuck all of your skirt well under you." He waited until she was settled then handed her a helmet. When she was securely on board, Alain maneuvered the big machine away from the curb and set off at a slow pace.

Eudora held loosely around his waist and kept her body rigidly upright. The thought of leaning against him flitted briefly through her mind then fluttered away on the breeze. The thought was too new—held too many uncertainties.

There were not a lot of motorcycle riders in Booneville, Mississippi, and she did not know anyone personally who owned one—they were not in her circle of friends. She smiled at the idea of how snobbish that sounded. It was followed by the thought that even though her parents had brought her up to be nonjudgmental and respectful of all people, her place in society had its limiting boundaries that might have in some way, contributed to her marrying Joel. The thought was tucked away for future examination.

———————

AFTER MOVING INTO THE COUNTRYSIDE, each curve, each rise and fall of the terrain brought scenic wonders. They skirted the city of Nimes. Alain had explored the area extensively when choosing where he wanted to establish residence. The city had history predating the Roman Empire. As landmarks or ruins became visible in the distance he thought again of man's place in the scheme of things. How fleeting his existence, but how enduring a few of his works.

He thought of the woman sitting stiffly behind him holding loosely around his waist. He was excited, yet recognized the need for caution. She had embraced his home unequivocally—he wanted her to share his love and appreciation for this land and its heritage. They had been traveling for two hours when he realized a break was needed, especially since they would be leaving the major road soon. When they approached a BP station, he pulled over.

———————

EUDORA WAS SO ENGROSSED IN the changing scenery she had barely become aware of the need for a rest stop. When Alain pulled into the gas station, she was ready for the break. He dismounted and extended his hand.

Eudora was surprised that her muscles had not stiffened too much during the ride—a few stretches would set things right. "What is this brand?" She was not familiar with the bright yellow and green BP sign.

"British Petroleum. It is one of the major brands here and very popular with tourists as their stores carry all sorts of snack items and souvenirs. We can have a few minutes to look around if you like. We still have about an hour and a half to ride. I should have asked if you were okay with a full day trip."

"A full day is fine, and I'll be quick, I promise." She smiled, wondering if he was thinking about the time frame involved when a woman promised to make it quick. True to her word, she used the facilities quickly, did a cursory survey of goods for sale, then made her way to the front of the store where he was waiting. He handed her a container he had filled with water and asked if she wanted anything else. She declined and they were once again on their way.

The narrower road was flanked by even more untamed landscape. Eudora liked the feeling of aloneness that crept in. They could be the last two people on the planet—it was their world. Barriers of tall trees would give way to shady glens where dwellings could be built. The solitary feeling was replaced by one of longing to make this their place—forever.

They reached the Gardon river and after following it briefly, the structure came into view. The Pont du Gard! Partially spanning the wide valley and river, it majestically stood, one of the manmade features that had defied time.

Alain parked away from the few other tourists in the area. He looked at Eudora and seeing the wonder in her eyes, simply took her hand and led her on a narrow path up a steep incline. A short climb brought them out atop the hill with a view of the valley. She stood, chin tilted upward to the breeze, then turned to face him.

"Thank you. I have never seen anything to match this. The age. In America we have structures that seem so old—they are young upstarts in comparison." She continued to look and assess the beauty and function of the aqueduct.

They sat on a small outcrop. Alain was in his element. "The top arches provided the means to bring water to Nimes. The lowest level was the road crossing the valley. When I sit here, I can imagine Caesar and his legion marching on this very road on their way to Rome. I haven't done any research on this, but it is logical that this is the route they would have taken."

"Why is there a wire across the top out there?" She indicated the barrier some distance out.

"Because there are people so foolish as to try to walk out a great distance on it. There are winds that sweep down the valley and could blow them right off. Protection for daredevils!"

Alain opened the small satchel he carried. *"Voila!* You thought I was going to starve you today, didn't you?"

Eudora laughed and denied the statement, but eagerly reached for the little flat box he handed her. It held a sandwich, vegetable sticks, dried fruit and a cookie. "Anna again, right?"

"What, you don't think I packed this myself?"

They both laughed, then ate in silence, each lost in thoughts of sorting feelings, possibilities.

"Tell me something about an event in your life, before you were married—before you met your husband."

Her fingers worried the fabric of her skirt as she gazed pensively into the distance. Retrieving a special memory. She looked up at him with a twinkle in her eyes and a mischievous smile lifted the corners of her mouth. "Well, it may sound silly to you, but the season of my debut was the last time I remember being truly happy. Mama and I spent hours, even days together. It was all so exciting to me—I would have been a complete mess without Mama's calm overseeing of every detail. Of course, she was in her element—completing my wardrobe, planning our ball. There were not a lot of lessons needed because I had taken ballet since I was five, so just some ballroom dance lessons were required to ensure that I wouldn't step on partners' toes. How to walk, how to sit, I learned from birth! How to make small talk was learned at the dinner table."

"Did you ever feel that everything was prescribed? Did you ever feel rebellious? Did you ever wonder if there was more?"

So many questions raised, so many details desired and she was eager to respond. "Not then, I truly didn't. Nothing felt forced—just natural growing up. My parents loved me—I had friends—there were activities. The only rebellion I ever indulged in was the silver pattern debacle—my mother would have used a more polite term." She laughed with the recollection.

Alain gave her a quizzical look. "Silver pattern?"

"Well, yes. For a Southern woman, silver is important. First, it must be real. You can fake a smile, you can dye your hair, but you must never have fake silver—no silver plate! Silver patterns are treated like the Holy Grail. If you are to inherit, then your pattern is chosen for you. I was doomed to Francis the First! There are at least ten pieces per setting, and each is laden with a fruit design. There are twenty-eight pieces of fruit on the knife handle alone!"

He laughed, his look incredulous. "You are kidding, aren't you?"

The look she gave him assured that there was no jest intended.

"Sorry. So, what was your act of rebellion?" By now this comedy had gained his interest.

"Well, when I did begin to take notice of silver patterns, I fell in love with Chantilly! A friend's mother had it. While it has a pretty decorative edge, there is not piece of fruit or a single flower on it. My mother was so proud of the fact that our Francis the First was fourth generation, that I expected her to be devastated when I told her that I wanted to start collecting Chantilly. But even a disappointment would have been voiced softly and never to remonstrate or elicit guilt. Although, I did feel guilty for a while." Eudora paused and looked at Alain. "How unbearably shallow you must find me."

He took her hand. "I find you breathtakingly beautiful and fascinating. I know now how you ride the distances on your bicycle so easily—those ballet lessons. And I love the silver story." The last statement accompanied by a glance to be sure that it had not offended. "Then what about the rest of the debut season?"

"There were parties, teas, and balls. All light, frivolous and fun. Late nights with girlfriends discussing gowns, food, decorations—and boys! Dancing and flirting with those boys. I really did enjoy it all—I really did. Then there was the night of my ball. Mother had outdone herself—everything was perfection—Daddy was pleased even though it had cost him a fortune.

"I had danced with practically every boy invited—and flirted—then late in the evening Joel Winningham claimed a dance. He led me onto the dance floor, smiled, looked into my eyes, told me how beautiful I looked—I did not know my world had ended at that moment!"

She paused and shivered. She looked away and was glad that he was quiet. "It's strange how your world can change, and you don't even know that it has. There's not a cloud in the sky, then suddenly there is a bolt of lightning, unexpected devastation that you cannot even comprehend, and you can only cower in a corner and hope to survive!"

She turned back to him and tears glistened in her eyes. The hopelessness in her voice matched the sadness on her face.

The conversation had certainly turned in an unintended direction. Reaching out to take both of her hands in his, he lifted them and pressed them to his chest. "Don't, Eudora, don't. Don't be sad, don't remember. It's gone—you told me it's gone, and the nightmare is over. Whatever the future is, it is not that. You have weathered that storm. It's passed." His tone was soothing, coaxing, pleading.

Her breathing slowed and her shoulders dropped. She raised her eyes to his, turned her hands to hold his, and smiled. "You're so right. There are bound to be memories of happy things that just lead right into those old hurts, so I have to learn where to cut them off, sort through—keep the good and discard the bad! Now, speaking of good, I want to thank you for bringing me to this beautiful place and for the history lesson." Freeing one of her hands, she swept it to indicate the vista below them.

Still clutching her other hand, he stood and helped her to her feet. "I suppose we had better start back. We'll take a slightly different route so that we will have different scenery."

With belongings packed up, they walked down the hill, mounted the bike, and headed back. Conversation being impossible, they rode with the hum of the motor and their own thoughts.

Eudora's thoughts were troubling. How could she feel what she was feeling? How could she tell if it was real? How could she be falling in love with a man she had just met—someone from another country—someone from such a different life and culture? Thinking was disturbing, detracting from her enjoyment of the ride, so she let her mind clear of all except appreciating the beauty of the countryside.

———————

ALAIN'S THOUGHTS WERE NO LESS conflicted. How to proceed. Slowly, quietly, gently. Anything else would frighten her—he was certain of that now. How to do that—when he wanted to hold her in his arms, brush away the hurt, and make the bad dreams disappear forever. When he so desperately needed to kiss her, make love to her. Reason reminded him, *slowly, quietly, gently.*

The beauty of this land—I gazed in awe at one scene after another—each beautifully unique.

CHAPTER 11

SHE RELAXED BUT STILL HELD his waist with minimum pressure and kept herself upright but not as stiffly. It was enough for now. The thought brought a smile. For now.

They made one brief stop to use the facilities and get bottles of water. She assured him that just a few minutes of walking around was all that would be needed to be ready for the rest of the trip.

As they reached the outskirts of *St. Rèmy,* she mused that the long trip had actually seemed quite short and was reluctant to have it end.

All too soon they pulled up in front of the hotel.

He came to a stop and let the bike idle. "There's no room to park here. We should be able to find a place around the corner then I can walk you in."

Before he could pull away, she placed a hand on his arm. "Really, you don't need to do that. I will just go in and straight to my room."

He nodded in agreement, turned off the motor and dismounted, then helped her off the bike, but continued to hold her hand.

"Thank you for a wonderful day. I cannot begin to tell you how much I enjoyed it." Unsaid words were tucked away to be saved for another time.

"You're very welcome—it was absolutely my pleasure." He paused, then seemed tentative. "Would you be interested in another trip tomorrow?"

"I'd love to." A blush accompanied the quick answer. He need not have worried that it was too soon.

"Same time tomorrow then." He dropped her hand, mounted and started the bike, and was gone. She watched until he was no longer in view before going into the hotel.

Though it was fairly early in the evening, the traveling, fresh air, and encompassing excitement of the day had caused her to be ready to retire early.

As she bathed, thoughts tried to crowd into her mind. Thoughts of him joining her there. Thoughts of him holding her to him, kissing her neck, her shoulder....

She hurried from the bath, toweled quickly, donned a nightgown, and slipped between the cool sheets. Now the invading thoughts were of him joining her there. "No." Spoken firmly. Pulling the cover up to her chin, she willed her mind blank. Fatigue was her ally, so sleep came in minutes.

She was not spared the nightmares, but there were also dreams of traveling through a fantasyland countryside where heroes chased away menacing dragons.

THE ALARM JARRED HER FROM deep sleep. Alarm? Why had she set an alarm? She practically jumped from the bed. There was an alarm because today she was going on another trip with Alain. Happy thoughts, tunes, and little scenarios flitted through her head during preparations for the day. Care was taken with appearance. Breakfast was eaten in the coffee shop—couldn't have a growling stomach, and dinner had been skipped the previous night. She was on the curb at fifteen minutes before nine—early!

In less than five minutes he pulled up—also early! Pleasantries exchanged, they were on their way. He had not mentioned a destination and she had not inquired.

Today he headed more south than west. The landscape was different and began to change quickly. They were skirting marshy lands that were the beginning of the Rhone delta. Riding close to shallow waters with tall reeds, they surprised marsh birds which rose with frantic flapping or graceful swoops.

Eudora had just noticed a misty cloud low lying on the distant horizon when Alain maneuvered the bike a little farther from the water's edge and parked with some of the taller grasses between them and the water. They dismounted, but before Eudora could question him, the scene unfolding grabbed her attention.

The mist rolled toward them. Eudora fell to her knees in awe as she recognized that at the head of the cloud was a galloping herd of horses. Alain dropped beside her, but she gave him only a glance before fixing her gaze upon the spectacle.

As if born of the mist, the herd was made up entirely of matched gray horses. They were not large animals, but their proportions were beautiful. She watched as the small herd and the mist they were kicking up passed by. Stunned into silence for moments, she turned to him with wonder in her eyes.

"Magnificent."

"Those are the wild horses of the Camargue. I was hoping we would see them today. That was a relatively small herd, but their presentation was perfect—a show just for you." He smiled as he looked at her.

The momentary spell broken, she found her voice, "How—why are they so perfectly matched like that—in the wild—no specialized breeding?"

"There were no young in that herd. If there had been, they would have been brown or black. The horses are all the same—they have black skin and are born with a black or brown coat. As they get older, all new hair is white. The white hair with the underlying black skin gives all of them the appearance of being gray."

She laughed. "I should have realized that you would know all about them. What else should I know about these horses—other than they are one of nature's marvels?"

"They are one of the oldest breeds in the world and no one is sure of their origin. They have the same genes as their ancestors, naturally breeding out man's attempt to infuse outside blood. They are used by cowboys who herd the bulls for bullfights."

A frown crossed her face at the mention of these beautiful animals being part of that blood sport.

"You should feel privileged. Not many tourists actually get to see the horses other than in romantic pictures of them."

"Romantic—yes, they are that. Ethereal, creatures appearing by magic from storied lands." She reached a hand to him as she started to stand, and he helped her to her feet.

"We'll just move farther back to where water won't seep up around us so we can have our lunch."

Anna had once again packed morsels fit for the gods. They were devoured by mortals in silence—silence in deference to the majesty of the land and the perfection of the day.

Alain noticed it first. A darkening on the horizon. "Uh-oh—we may have lingered too long. The weather forecast mentioned that there might be showers tonight, but from the looks of that, they could be moving in earlier than expected."

They were on their way almost at once. As they headed northward, the sky darkened with alarming speed. Oddly enough, Eudora was not concerned—Alain would be in control of the situation and would take care of her. Take care of her—a new thought and sensation to add to her growing repertoire. It felt good—it felt safe.

She figured they were more than halfway back when it began. It was a slow gentle rain, not pelting, but they were soon soaked to the skin.

Eudora sensed a change in direction but was surprised at rounding a curve and seeing the cottage a short distance ahead. Alain pulled the bike into the open front of a small outbuilding. He dismounted and turned to her.

"I am so sorry. I should have been prepared. We should have taken the car, or I should at least have brought rain ponchos. I knew this shortcut to my property where we could get inside and dry much more quickly than going on to the city."

The smile she turned to him took him by surprise. "I haven't melted, have I? Must not be made of sugar! I wouldn't have missed today if I'd had to ride in the rain another hour."

He slipped an arm around her waist to guide her as they made a dash for the front door. Once inside, Eudora looked in dismay as water pooled at their feet.

"Don't worry. Stone floors are not damaged by water. Hang on just a minute." He disappeared into the powder room and emerged with a handful of small towels. "We can soak enough of the water off us to make a run for the bathrooms upstairs. Just follow me."

She wiped as much water as she could from her legs and wrung out her skirt-tail in one of the towels. Alain nudged her and set off, fairly running up the stairs. She kept pace with him, and both were laughing hysterically when they reached the top. A short distance down the upper hallway he flung open a door and bolted through with her following closely. She was barely aware of passing through a bedroom before following him through the next door into a spacious bathroom.

"Ah, tile floor—no more water worry." She leaned against an antique cabinet which held the sink.

"I'll wipe the wood floors as I leave. I'll put a robe outside the bedroom door for you to put on after showering. You should get into a good warm shower right away—it isn't really cold, but you don't want to chance catching a chill. Bring your clothes down with you and we can put them in the dryer."

Left alone, Eudora looked at the rest of the room. Modern and period elements had been carefully blended. The room had an old-world look, but the shower was thoroughly modern. She turned the water to warm then stripped down, putting her clothing into the sink. The warm spray soothed her. A niche in the tile wall held shampoo, conditioner, and soap, all smelling of lavender.

"Alain, Alain, Alain." The name whispered and repeated over and over. There was no use trying to keep denying—she loved him. It made no sense, it was improbable. But there it was.

Shaking herself back to reality, she turned off the water, found thick towels in the chest under the sink and rubbed herself until her skin glowed. With another towel wrapped around her and one around her hair, she opened the door and peeked out into the bedroom. Crossing to the hallway door, she found the robe lying folded just outside as promised.

The old, soft flannel was obviously one of his. Once it was overlapped and tied securely around her, she retrieved her clothing from the sink and wrapped everything in one of the heavy towels then headed downstairs. At the bottom, she stopped and stared. A small fire was blazing in the huge stone fireplace. In front of it, he had placed a low table surrounded by large pillows. Its surface was laden with a variety of dishes, some covered but sending out mouth-watering smells.

"Madam, a humble repast awaits." His smile was dazzling.

"Good grief! You have been busy. Surely I didn't take that long." She noticed that he was casually dressed in jeans and a well-worn shirt. When he stepped forward to take her bundle of clothes, there was the fresh scent of soap.

"Not long at all. Anna, bless her, had things organized to just heat a few minutes or remove covers and set out. I'll just put these things into the dryer and be right back."

She blushed at her admiration when watching him leave the room. He moved with the grace of someone at home in his own skin. Observing a man in this way was entirely new to her. Oh, she had felt stirrings, but never anything like this raw desire when looking at him. More and more there was realization of how naïve she was—how blithely unaware of how a relationship between a man and woman could be.

"Are you ready to sample more of Anna's wonders?" Entering the room quietly, taking her by surprise, Eudora jumped at his greeting.

"Absolutely."

They sat on the pillows and leisurely enjoyed the various offerings. Having eaten their fill, Alain had one final surprise. A glazed pot held hot chocolate which had cooled to perfect drinking temperature.

Eudora licked her lips and felt like a contented cat licking its whiskers. She decided purring would be out of the question but smiled at the thought.

"A penny for your thoughts."

She smiled at him. "They involve cats and cream and purring."

He laughed. "I think that's a good thing." His face turned serious. "I don't want to overstep here, but it's late, it's still raining—we could take the car, but if you want to stay, that guest room is available—just a guest room for the night."

Seeing his concerned look, she stood and reassured him that she understood his offer. "Thank you. I'll see you in the morning."

He jumped to his feet. "I think you will find everything you need in the room, but if you need anything at all, my room is at the end of the hall." Again, his look was one of the *damned foot in the mouth*.

"Thank you. Good night." She climbed the stairs, afraid to look back. Afraid for him to see what was on her face. Afraid she would not have the resolve to finish the trek to the guest room.

The beauty of this land calls to me—is it only the land...?

CHAPTER 12

EUDORA COULD NOT JUDGE HOW long she had been in bed. Sleep evaded her as scenes from the day kept running in a never-ending loop through her mind. Alain had come up the stairs shortly after she retired. His steps had moved straight down the hall and there was the sound of a door closing.

She got up and went to the bathroom for a glass of water. Staring back from the mirror over the sink was the face of a stranger. Hair, while not tangled, was disheveled. Eyes were wide, holding unaccustomed desire. Lips full and parted—waiting to be kissed? She pressed her hand to her chest as if to quiet her fluttering heart. Invading thoughts and feelings terrified her— she ran back to the bed determined to sleep.

Had she dozed? Something caught her ear—a soft footfall outside the door? It was not locked—not that she would have wanted it to be. Lying quietly, she could barely feel the rise and fall of her chest. He was there— she knew he was. An eternity passed—afraid he would come in—afraid he wouldn't. Was that the sound of his breathing or was it only the echo of her own? A faint shuffle and she knew he was gone. A tear slid onto the pillow as sleep finally came.

ALAIN STARED INTO THE FIRE, willing himself not to turn around as Eudora climbed the stairs. After a few minutes, he carried the remains of the meal into the kitchen, refrigerated leftovers, put dishes into the dishwasher, then went slowly up the stairs. He did not pause when passing the guest room door.

He undressed and climbed into bed, but restless tossing left him, once again, hopelessly tangled in the sheets. Kicking his legs free, sitting on the side of the bed with shoulders sagging and head bowed, he put his hands to his face. The mind refuses to let go of things imprinted indelibly upon it. Eudora was imprinted. His love for her was imprinted. His desire for her was imprinted. A glance at the clock on the bedside table told him that he should have been asleep an hour ago. He noticed that the ring that had been lying there was gone. A quick search under the table and the general vicinity did not produce it. Anna must have put it away in a drawer—he must remember to ask her about it.

He stared at the door. Moving slowly and carefully, he opened it. The walk down the hall was noiseless until he was a silent specter standing outside her room. His body was silent, but an inner battle raged. To go to her or to not go to her. A *Hamlet*-like analogy pierced the conflict and brought a fleeting smile to his lips. A momentary respite from turmoil. No sound came from the other side of the door. Nothing to guide him to a decision.

Minutes passed. He placed his hand on the door, bowed his head, then returned to his room. Sleep eluded him for a while but when it came, so did the nightmares. They were the same torture and terror that now haunted him nightly.

————————

EUDORA WOKE TO THE SMELLS of bacon and coffee. Sunlight slanted through sheer white curtains. She lazily stretched her legs, then her arms. This new feeling of contentment brought a smile to her lips. Sitting up, she looked around the room. The décor matched the cottage—dark wood floor, antique bed and armoire, comfortable period chair placed near the window.

She stretched once more when she stood up. The robe had to be adjusted as it had been slept in. She completed her trip to the bathroom with a splash of cold water to her face then opened the door to the hallway and found her clothes neatly folded.

Dressed for the day and bounding down the stairs, she nearly collided with Alain who was just about to come up.

"Whoa! I take it you slept well and are gloriously reenergized." His laugh was contagious.

"Absolutely. Anyone would be reenergized by the smells wafting up the stairs. I assume the legendary Anna is involved here."

"Actually, no. The legendary Anna had some business to take care of, so we are on our own. The magnificent Alain has prepared an offering for madam's approval."

She laughed, "Approval granted, oh my, yes." The kitchen table was laden with eggs, bacon, and a fresh fruit salad. She took the chair indicated, reached for the steaming cup of coffee and sipped. "This coffee alone will get you a five-star rating!"

Small talk reviewing the previous day carried them through breakfast. Each seemed to be waiting to follow the other's lead. Alain broke the stalemate. "What about today? Do you want to spend it here?" His tone was light.

"I think I would like to go back to the hotel." She noted the brief downcast look that crossed his face. "But just to freshen up and get my paints. I feel like painting. I'm seeing the entire region in a new light. I know now why I was not very happy with the work I have done so far—it has no life, no feeling—I have that to inject now. Take me back and I'll meet you at *our spot,*" smiling as she emphasized the words, "in about two hours."

"Deal. Shall we take the car, or will you brave the bike again?"

"Oh, most definitely the bike. Believe it or not, I really did not mind the rain. The two days in the country were fabulous—unique experiences that I will always treasure. When I have those feelings about a place or experience, I am humbled, knowing how privileged I was to have been given that. I always know they will never be repeated, at least not in that exact manner—maybe never duplicated is more accurate."

They were soon on their way with the motorcycle humming along, and the gentle wind in their faces. Eudora sat upright as before but she was not looking at the scenery sliding by. She saw his hair curling below the helmet. She saw strong thighs as they gripped the bike. She saw broad shoulders tapering down to the narrow waist her arms encircled. Nature could not distract her thoughts today, at least not scenic nature. Only the nature of a man calling to a woman filled her eyes with the beauty of him, her nostrils with the scent of him, and her touch with a desire for him. She tightened her arms around him, tentatively lay her head against his back, then totally surrendered and snuggled close to him.

ONLY BY SHEER WILLPOWER AND concentration did Alain avoid swerving off the road. It was all he could do to keep from stopping to take her in his arms. She had dropped a barrier. The rest of the ride would give them time to absorb this and think about the next step. He arched his back slightly against her to acknowledge her move. When she adjusted her arms even more securely and rubbed her cheek against his back, then lay there quietly, he curbed the urge to shout in exaltation but could not control the thoughts of all the possibilities that stretched before them.

When they pulled to a stop in front of the hotel, neither moved. Both were reluctant to abandon the closeness so recently established. With a sigh, he gave her a hand to dismount, then swung off and turned to face her. Neither tried to hide what showed on their faces. She handed her helmet to him. He reached out and brushed a strand of hair from her face. Lips were moistened but words were slow to form.

"I'll hurry."

"I'll be waiting," he replied.

SHE COULD SEE HIM—A tiny speck in the distance. She watched him grow nearer and nearer as her speed increased. She stopped a few feet from him.

Her breathing was labored from the hurried ride. "I'm here."

"Yes. You are." In two strides, he was beside her and as he clutched her to him, the bicycle fell into the grass. Their eyes locked. He bent his lips to hers and tasted heaven. He did manage enough thought to feel the need for restraint, but that was ripped away when arms wrapped around his neck and her body melded to his. Their kiss deepened and their desire flamed. Neither had any idea of how much time passed before they were able to tear themselves apart.

He shook his head slowly from side to side as he looked into her face. "I love you—I love you—I love you—I can't stop saying that."

"And I don't want you to stop—ever. I love you, Alain. I love you, too." They kissed again and again. Feelings denied bubbled to the surface and swept them into a raging current.

When they were able to end the kiss, they stood holding each other in an embrace meant never to be broken. He looked down into her eyes. "You need time—I understand that. I have waited for you from the first moment I saw you—I can wait longer. It has to be your decision."

"You're right. I do need time to think, but right now all I can do is feel." Stepping away from him, she picked up supplies from the bicycle. "I want to paint you!"

"What?" His look was one of surprise.

She gave him a playful push. "You sit right over there—just so—there. The light is perfect. I can't promise how good it will be, but I want to paint your portrait."

He laughed at the idea but sat as asked.

Paint was applied quickly, colors in broad strokes to capture the essence of him, then smaller details were added. Sunlight highlighted his hair and the planes of his cheekbones. His aquiline nose and strong chin proved easy to complete. The artist caught the sparkle of his gray-green eyes. Marveling at how quickly the work progressed came with the realization that it was the love going into very stroke that brought success.

Alain took advantage of an interruption when the artist stepped back to look at her work. "Do you realize you have been doing this for two hours? Your model needs a break, lady." He laughed and stepped toward her.

She stepped around the easel and put herself between him and his obvious destination. "Absolutely no peeking at this until I have finished it." Eudora joined his laughter. "Surely it has not been two hours," but a look at her watch validated his statement. "I just have a few finishing touches to add that I can do later."

Producing containers of water from a backpack, he offered her one. He took it from her when she finished and dropped it to the ground, then took her in his arms. They kissed—tenderly at first—then their passion could not be denied. The kiss was reluctantly broken, and he tucked her head under his chin. She knew he could feel her heart beating against his chest as she could hear his pounding in her ear.

"Are you coming home with me?"

"I can't. I want to, but I can't. Do you understand?" There was a hint of pleading in her voice.

He rubbed her back and whispered against her hair, "I do. It's okay, it's okay. I love you. I want everything to be right for you. I will never ask you to compromise."

"It's not a matter of compromise. I love you. There are just some things I have to sort out with no distractions."

He held her away from him and gave her a mock grave look. "Are you insinuating that I am a distraction?"

"No sir, flat out saying it!"

"Tomorrow?"

"Absolutely. Right here." She couldn't think about tomorrow—not anything concrete anyway. Tomorrow would bring more—more what? More—whatever it was. The thought caught her breath. Pack up things—hands had to be kept busy or they would reach for him again. The feelings were as tangible as if the touch was real—feelings of running fingers through his hair, tracing the cheekbones with her fingers, tentatively touching his lips—replacing that touch with her lips.

Jerked back to reality, Eudora attached her supplies to the bike as he held it upright for her. Stepping onto riding position only left time for him to brush her lips lightly with his before she set off.

There was a freedom traveling on the motorcycle with no barrier between us. With the sun on our faces, we were alone in those hours of tranquility.

I was very self-conscious reaching around him. My feelings were so conflicted—so overwhelming. I rubbed the wedding ring on my finger. Before God had I promised to love and be bound to another forever.

But that was not enough. When I began painting his portrait, all was lost—or gained. The love of my life had been revealed to me. I could not imagine a future that did not include him—it need only be planned and then held close—and lived.

CHAPTER *13*

SHE SAT STARING OUT THE window without seeing, mind blank, not making progress. The time had come. Decisions must be made. Logical thinking must be done—it was time. They loved each other. There must be a future for them. It had not been put into words, but it was written in their hearts. And now—she must make a decision. What were her choices? She could simply stay here, be with him, take one day at a time and put off other decisions until later.

She would have to give her parents an immediate explanation, of course, even though she was sure Joel would have given them a plausible story. They would be hurt that she had not said goodbye before leaving. She would need to contact them soon. She felt more than a little guilt for the worry she knew she had caused them, but her flight had been for her life. There had not been time to think and prepare—escape had to be immediate. As for her marriage, Joel would not let her just disappear—she must deal with him. She would have to go home and get a divorce as quickly and quietly as possible.

Muffled organ music coming from the church across the street broke into her thoughts. The famous organ of St. Martin. She picked up a sweater and went down the stairs.

She exited the hotel and crossed the street to the church.

The interior was cool and dim. Eudora sat on one of the back pews and noted that there was no one else inside. It was disappointing that much too soon the organist completed his practice, and now she sat in silence while shadows pressed around her, comforting in a way. Religion was more or less a routine to the Winninghams. They attended Sunday services and Eudora participated in the ladies' activities—just what was expected of them. Sitting in the silence and beauty of this ancient structure gave new meaning to it all—solace and guidance.

"Be still and know that I am God." Eudora remembered the verse. *Still* was that all that could be managed at this moment. How to pray? Pray for what? Permission to break her wedding vows? Permission to love a man who was not her husband? Peace? Calm for a troubled soul? For the first time in her life, Eudora felt spirituality in a personal way and prayed as never before.

Outside, shadows lengthened as the supplicant inside stilled in mind and spirit. The woman who left the church and entered the hotel was prepared to face the days ahead, ready to begin to make decisions and plans.

Tea and a croissant in the coffee shop was all she was able to manage for dinner. Once upstairs, physical and mental fatigue demanded the comfort of the bed. It felt good to lie down and pull covers over her tired body, but sleep was not part of the bargain. There was no tossing and turning, but plans made and discarded filled the night.

In the hours just before dawn, Eudora reached a decision and found peace. Finally, all thoughts of logic and improbability had been put aside. She loved him. She loved him as surely as she breathed—loving him was that essential. And she knew with certainty that he loved her. She could see it in his eyes and feel it in his touch. His gaze filled with awe when he looked at her, a look that told her of the value he placed upon her. In his eyes she was more precious than anything that could be imagined. And when he touched her—the tenderness, the respect, the desire to protect, the need to love her, were apparent.

He was everything she dreamed or imagined that a man could or should be. He was the prince in the fairy tale, the knight in shining armor—what a Southern woman was raised to believe the man she married would be. He was everything she had been taught to desire and expect. He was everything her husband was not.

WHEN THE SUN ROSE, EUDORA left her bed with her course set. Dressed with care in the flowing white dress she wore that first day when he had sat in the distance watching her paint, she came to this spot before the last of the dew had even gone. She ignored the wet hem of her skirt dragging around her legs. It would dry later in the morning sunlight. Walking rather than riding the bicycle had given her more time to think, to prepare what to say, yet knowing that at first sight of him anything planned would be forgotten. The only thing important in that moment would be to hasten into his arms.

ALAIN QUICKENED HIS PACE. SHE had to be there—he would not allow for the possibility that she would not be in the exact spot where he had first seen her, first knew that he loved her beyond all reason.

He stopped, his heart racing more from anticipation or anxiety than the fast pace he had set. And then the fears, the doubts, the hopeless longings all melted away. She was standing with her arms folded, looking toward the village. It was then she turned and looked in his direction.

SHE KNEW HE WOULD COME—midmorning at least. He would have no reason to think she would be here this early. No, that was not true. She knew that he would come, and just as surely, that he would have no doubt of finding her here.

He was here—she knew it before turning around. And he was there in the distance, beginning to run toward her. Uttering a small cry, she flew toward him. When they were a dozen feet apart, she suddenly stopped, and he halted in response. With head bowed and a tear rolling down her cheek, Eudora moved forward with slow measured steps, approached him, wrapped her arms around him, and resting her head on his chest whispered, "I'm home."

His arms went around her, offering protection, welcoming her home. After his shirt was wet with her tears, she raised her face and offered her lips.

His gentle kiss deepened as she slid her arms around his neck and pressed against him. With a low moan he ran the tip of his tongue across her lips and as they opened to him, he explored the velvety recesses within. As passion stirred them, she gently put her hands on his biceps and pushed herself away to look into his face. When they looked into each other's eyes, neither had doubts as to what was desired.

"If the laws of God and man are to be broken, Alain, I want it to be with the clear understanding of what we want from each other." He must not have any doubt that she was offering equal responsibility for the breaking of marriage vows and offering herself completely and without reservation.

He held her gently. "I want to love you as you deserve to be loved, to show you how a man loves a woman he values above all else. I want my body to show you what is in my heart. I want to love you now—if that's what you want, too."

She slid her fingers down his arms until they rested in his hands and he held them firmly as she sank toward the bed of grass and flowers. With deft movements he retrieved a blanket from the pack he carried. It billowed in the breeze as it was spread, and he lifted her onto it. He knelt beside her and began to show her the love and adoration of which he spoke.

He loved her with gentleness and tenderness, teaching her body that any pain should be only that of exquisite peaks of desire that resulted in exaltation upon release. He whispered to her of her beauty, his desire for her, his pleasure in her, and his love for her.

She received his body and his love with no reservations, and as their passion mounted, tradition and conventions were stripped away. She responded to him and loved him unfettered by rules or guilt. They loved each other, giving and taking pleasure, racing toward fulfillment, then pulling back. Unable to wait longer, they cried each other's names as completion overwhelmed them. He held her close and told her of his love and her perfection. She sighed with contentment as he wrapped his arms around her to shelter her as they rested.

The sun wrapped them in a cocoon of warmth, having dried the last vestiges of dampness from the early morning.

Eudora propped on one elbow to look at him, fascinated that she took such joy in looking at his body, which again reacted to her gaze.

"Madam, you are going to cause me to blush if you keep looking at me like that," he teased. But it was she who reddened and looked away. The breeze cooled their passion-heated bodies and choreographed a ballet of flowers around them. In the ensuing silence, Eudora knew that she was no longer the woman who had run away. She was the woman who had found her way.

She looked back at him, cheeks washed of anything akin to embarrassment and as her gaze swept over his body, she said, "I guess I truly am a wanton woman—to have behaved like that, to take so much joy from looking at you. But if that's what I am, right now that is the most delicious thing I can think of to be." Her eyes held his and her transformation was apparent. Her soft Southern drawl and her words fueled the fire within him.

He laughed and pulled her on top of him. "As long as you're my woman." And he accompanied her in practicing her newfound wantonness.

Bodies satiated, wrapped in each other's arms, they lay looking at the sky that was now bluer and filled with clouds they identified as castles and unicorns. He pointed skyward, "Look, there's a motorcycle." Following the direction of his long, tapered finger, she squinted at the cloud formation that in no way resembled a motorcycle. Of course, the castles and unicorns had been stretches too.

"Alain Philidor, motorcycles do not fit in with castles and unicorns." She looked and saw the smile curling his lips and crinkling the corners of his eyes. "You are a tease." As she turned her gaze from his face, her eyes made contact with his arousal, she admitted defeat and with mock pleading, begged him to love her again. This time, their energy drained and their minds filled only with images and thoughts of the other, they drifted to sleep wrapped in each other's arms.

Alain woke first. He lay quietly so as not to disturb her. The perfume of the crushed lavender mingling with her fragrance and the scent of him on her made an intoxicating combination. Having arranged her dress carefully over her, he looked back to her face to find her staring at him. "I was afraid you might be chilled," he offered.

"And covering me with my dress was the best idea you could come up with?" Both laughed as he rolled over to cover her with his body. Laughter was quelled with kisses. This was leisurely, a time for exploring, a time to tempt, a time to learn, a time to excite—a time to shudder together then lie entwined until the breeze actually was becoming cooler.

"You know, we do have to move and get up." His voice did not hold much conviction.

This was met with a small groan and unopened eyes. "Uh-uh. I don't want to move—I want to stay right here."

"Well, it won't be nearly so romantic to wake up dew soaked and shivering cold." He gathered her into a sitting position and kissed her throat, then each eyelid until both fluttered open.

"Then take me home."

The words cut him to the quick—then he saw the look in her eyes, and she said, "Home is where you are." He started gathering clothing quickly— quickly because if they did not get dressed and leave now, they would be here until morning.

"Come live with me and be my love...."

CHAPTER 14

THE JOURNEY TO THE COTTAGE took an inordinate amount of time. There were pauses for kissing, for touching, for looking. They held hands, but sometimes that was not enough. Eventually, despite such distractions, they reached the garden.

"Wait." Rather than entering the door to the kitchen, he led her around the house and opened the heavy wooden door at the front. He scooped her into his arms, carried her inside and headed directly up the wide staircase. "We're home."

"I love the sound of that."

He set her down in front of the door to his bedroom and gave her a questioning look.

She laughed, "You have to ask? After spending all day making love?"

His laughter joined hers, "Just giving you one last chance, woman."

"Woman—*your* woman." Reaching down, Eudora opened the door then lifted her face to meet his lips.

He groaned, grasped her tightly around the waist to lift her from the floor then carried her to the bed. He placed her there gently, but gentleness quickly turned to urgency. Urgency became unrestrained abandonment. Time did not exist until much later.

"Goodnight, my darling girl. I don't want to let go of you even for a moment, but I have to sleep."

She could not even manage a clever retort as her eyes were already half closed. "I love you," her voice trailed off.

They slept deeply, untroubled with nothing left unsaid.

Moonlight was streaming through the window when Eudora woke ravenous. She had eaten nothing yesterday and was relatively sure that Alain hadn't either. Telling herself that food could wait until breakfast didn't work. A growl from her stomach would soon be accompanied by more hunger noises and then he would wake up. A smile curled her lips—he would wake up. Making love with stomachs growling didn't sound that romantic, so a plan formed. That refrigerator had plenty of food and that pantry was no doubt well stocked. Bring up a tray—food for the stomach, then....

Alain never moved a muscle as Eudora eased from the bed. Clothing was piled in a heap on the floor. She picked up his shirt and held it to her face to inhale the scent of him. She slid her arms into the sleeves and wrapped it around her body, then shivered with a sense of urgency to fulfill her mission and return. She stole quietly down the stairs and hurried to the kitchen.

A tray on the counter began filling up—fruit, cheese, and there would definitely be tea and crackers in the pantry. She hummed as she went about her task.

As the door to the pantry swung open, the pages fluttered on the calendar hanging inside. A glance noted that it was the end of June—she had been in *St. Rèmy* a month already.

Suddenly, Eudora froze. A chill ran over her entire body. Time stopped. The month was June—the date at the top was 2006! It must be some sort of joke. Grabbing the calendar from the door, her frantic fingers flipped through pages looking for some reason why it had this date—this impossible date. She flipped through the pages again. Her mind would not focus.

The chill persisted, joined by tingling, then numbness. What was this? Uncertainty began somewhere deep in the pit of her stomach and sent tentacles of fear reaching for her heart. Surely a mistake of some sort. Coherent thought was becoming more and more difficult. She looked at the shelves stocked with packages and cans of food. 2006—the numbers jumped out at her from a line of numbers written across the top of a bag of coffee. What was that?

She picked up a can of peas—2007—these along with numbers that looked to represent months and days. Picking items off the shelf then discarding each for another made no difference—they all conspired to confirm that horrible story that mocked her from the calendar.

Incredulous! Disbelief.

How could this be? This impossibility?

Her brain wouldn't function. No thoughts were there. She was smothering, couldn't breathe—she must wake up. She was awake.

Fleeing the pantry, she started for the stairs—what could she say? He would think she was crazy. Think—it was difficult to think when breathing was almost impossible. Changing direction, the back door became her destination. A few more steps and she was out into the garden. No easier to breathe! It was a world of black and white. Moonlight silvered the roses and the water splashing in the fountain.

Moonlight—flowers—water—thought, there needed to be thought. Alain would help her to understand—he had to. Thought—she had to stay here with him. No wildly skewed time could keep them apart. "I have to stay!" She twisted the wedding ring on her finger until it came off. "I have to stay!" She hurled the ring into the darkness—darkness that seemed to shatter into pieces—the pieces gather around her—engulfing her.

There was a roar of wind rushing through trees. Clouds obscured the moonlight. The earth was spinning. Her head was spinning. Nothing was real. She must be dreaming. But she wasn't dreaming.

Eudora felt herself slipping to the ground—the ground which was covered with tall grass and brambles reaching out to pull at her as she fell.

ALAIN GRADUALLY ROSE TO CONSCIOUSNESS. With eyes still closed and a smile on his lips, he reached a hand to the other side of the bed. Empty. Evidently Eudora was already up and about. A trip to the bathroom did not reveal a trace of her. He pulled on jeans and called her name as he went down the stairs.

She was not in the kitchen or the garden. Puzzled, he went back to the bedroom. Her clothes were gone. She would be at *their* place waiting for him. The thought of a repeat of yesterday made him smile. He dressed quickly and was on his way.

She was not there, nor by the stream—there was no place left to look.

Concern turned to panic. Back at the cottage he picked up the telephone. The conversation left him staring blankly at the instrument in his hand. What was going on? Nothing of what he had heard made any sense. He drove to the village.

————————————

ANNA WAS BESIDE HERSELF. ALAIN had been gone for four days. She had been unable to reach him at any of the locations she thought he might be. Calling anyone to look for him could cause embarrassment. Had he been called away on business, or on a trip with his new love? It wasn't like him not to leave a note or call her. There wasn't much more busy work that she could create to occupy her hands and certainly not her mind. What might have been the hundredth time looking out of the window brought success. She dried her hands on a towel, then rushed out the door.

Alain sat at the table under the tree. His face was expressionless and his eyes blank. He obviously hadn't shaved for days. His clothes were rumpled and none too clean.

"I didn't hear your car. Have you been in an accident? Where have you been? Are you hurt? Alain, what is wrong?" Anna could not keep the questions from tumbling out. Getting no answers, she placed her hand on his, "Alain, what is wrong? Are you ill?"

"She's gone." The voice was cold, without feeling.

"Who is gone? What are you talking about?"

"Eudora. She's gone. Disappeared."

"People don't just disappear. Have you tried calling her hotel?"

"I called her hotel—I was told that no one named Eudora Winningham had ever been registered there."

"There must have been some mistake. Maybe you were mistaken about where she was staying." Anna was shaking her head. How strange.

"I went there—I questioned the staff. She was never there. Then I remembered I had always picked her up in front of the hotel. I have checked every hotel in the city—she was never in any of them. I couldn't think of any reason for her not telling me where she was staying. Then I thought maybe a bed and breakfast, but no luck there either. Then I checked the hospitals and the police department asking if there had been an American woman in an accident. None had seen an American woman alone.

"I finally was desperate enough to make calls to America—Booneville, Mississippi. Telephone listings—there was no Joel or Eudora Winningham listed! None in all of Mississippi!"

Anna sat across from him in disbelief. There had to be an explanation. A seed of doubt crept in. She had never seen this woman. Alain had been so distraught over Lauren. Could he have had some sort of breakdown? No, not possible. He had been so happy, so *changed*. Her heart broke—the devastation left by Lauren was nothing compared to what she was witnessing now.

Rising to put her arm around his shoulders brought no response.

"I have to face the fact that she lied about everything, who she was— everything. I cannot even venture a reason as to why."

———————

WITHOUT EVEN ACKNOWLEDGING THE COMFORTING arm around his shoulders, he rose, walked through the house, and went straight to his bedroom. It was cleaned and in order. Of course it was, Anna had been here working. The bed was smooth, sterile, no sign of them having been there sharing love that both had promised would last forever. Without bothering to undress, he lay down, not sure he could sleep in this bed. When he rolled onto his side, he noticed the ring on the bedside table—Anna must have found it. He picked it up—the inscription mocked him. He sent it hurling across the room—flung into the oblivion that had swallowed him.

Oblivion—limbo—where nothing real existed. She had been *real*—she had been in his arms—she was in his mind, his soul. There were so many questions, but only one had any validity—how could he survive, much less move on with his life?

Not one day at a time—not even one minute at a time—just take the next second's breath. Just not think of her in that breath. Just not see her face just not remember loving her.

———————

ALAIN SAT AT THE OLD table under the tree and looked over his domain. What did it have to offer? The beauty of the day was superficial. The blue sky with the white clouds could turn to black at any given time. Many of the flowers dancing in the breeze were in their death throes and with their going, the glory of their color and perfume would become a memory when covered in snow, their dead stems whipped by winter winds. Nothing lasted—nothing. The house, which he had found rotting and had lovingly restored, would fall into ruin again.

Unable to sit longer, he strode in the direction of the meadow. He had found her there, they had first made love there, perhaps some miracle would bring her there today. He did not really believe that. It was just one more hopeless random thought that ran through his mind.

The field was, as he knew it would be—without the departed artist. He looked around as he stood in the area where he had been when he first saw her, then where they had made love. The flowers and grass, revived, were springing back to their upright stance with only a few broken stems left as reminders of bodies pressing them down, dancing atop them. He threw himself on the ground as though crushing the plants once more could reverse the nightmare of the past few days.

He lay back and closed his eyes. As a breeze touched his face, he looked skyward. Two short-toed eagles danced in the air high above. Their swoops and passes, ascents and dives were a show that abruptly ended as one suddenly leveled off, and with strongly beating wings, flew determinedly away.

A mind can be slow to admit defeat. He rose and with feet of lead continued the hopeless journey. He did not find her by the stream where her laugh had rivaled the music of the rippling water. He remembered her skirt circling around her on the grass, then breaching that perimeter or rather eventually having been invited inside it. His body cried out as he remembered the silkiness of her skin, the fullness of her lips, the passion of her body responding to his.

He roared his pain to the heavens. He screamed his anger into the wind. He fell to his knees and lifting his face to the sun, let it create minute rainbows in the tears cascading down his cheeks.

Stumbling to his feet, he ran. His legs pumped until pain seared his muscles, and still he did not slow his pace. Crashing through the door, he once again threw his body in front of the piano. New music came pouring out. Quiet, infinitely tender, unbearably painful, then to a crashing discordant crescendo. As the last notes quivered to silence, "Eudora!" Souls tortured in hell heard the name that reverberated to every corner of the house.

Head bowed and arms hanging limply at his sides, he ascended the stairs. It was not toward heaven but the hell of a once again solitary bed.

ANNA SAT HUDDLED IN A corner in the kitchen. Alain had stormed into the house and passed without seeing her. She had started to follow him, but then had come the music. The tears began with the tender parts that told her that he had once again entrusted his heart into another's keeping. His love was there in every note, every nuance of phrasing. His destruction was there in the discordant minor key that followed. She was sobbing by the time the music stopped and lost her breath at the name echoing from the stone walls.

She had never met the woman who brought renewed happiness and renewed devastation.

...the devil you know....

CHAPTER 15

"WELL, LOOK WHAT THE CAT dragged in." Joel Winningham stopped short when he saw his wife sitting at the table in the breakfast room.

Eudora looked up but did not further acknowledge his presence.

He filled a plate from the covered dishes on the sideboard and set that, along with coffee at the opposite end of the table. "Well, would you like to tell me where you have been?"

Calm eyes were lifted to stare at him. "France."

"Doing what?"

"Painting, sightseeing."

"Do you plan to elaborate on anything or stick with as few words possible, as usual?" Had she always been this annoying, or was it something new? "When did you get back?"

"I came back early last evening. You were out. I slept in the guest room. I'll be moving my things in there later today."

He set the coffee down and stared at her. Something was different. Better put a stop to this right now. "I would have expected you to look rested, refreshed—too bad that doesn't seem to be the case." Criticism had always shaken her confidence. It was one of the main weapons in his arsenal. He was beginning to seethe inside—this attitude after she had been gone for weeks? Left him to explain her absence? Caused him to have to concoct some elaborate story to save embarrassment?

"Actually, the whole experience was very invigorating."

These clipped answers were becoming maddening. He cocked his head and raised one eyebrow.

"Well, what about the painting? When can I see the masterpieces?" This homecoming was not going exactly as he had envisioned.

"Actually, there was nothing worth bringing back. I left the canvases, but brought the memories." Was there something wistful in her voice?

Joel stared at his wife. What had made this change in her? This was not the soft spoken, compliant woman who had left here a few weeks ago. Her voice was still quiet, but now there was a sharpness in her tone, a defiance in her eyes. He carefully folded his napkin, scooted back his chair, and stood, never taking his eyes off of her.

"If you come near me, I will scream. The staff will hear. You will never again hit me without repercussions. I will charge you with abuse. I will divorce you and humiliate you as much as possible. I have always kept quiet. I always hoped your promises to change were true. I know now that you are nothing but a bully and a sadist. Keeping me quiet was as thrilling to you as the actual hitting. You are sick. Any scandal will not be as awful to deal with as staying with you."

Her voice was cold, matter-of-fact, devoid of emotion... and held a resolve he had never heard before. The look in her eyes matched the tone of her voice.

He hated her at that moment. She would have to be made to pay. He walked slowly past her and out of the room. A plan for what to do about this must be decided—quickly.

EUDORA WAS QUIVERING, BUT CONGRATULATED herself on her bravado. He had backed down. It would be foolish, however, to think he was beaten. Constant vigilance would be needed. The first thing to do was find a lawyer. Joel would buy her silence with a divorce. She would have to tell her parents. She walked to the phone. "Mama, it's Eudora. Well, I'm truly sorry I worried you and Daddy, but I really needed some time away. I'm sure Joel explained." He would have made up a good story to save face.

"If you and Daddy don't have plans for this afternoon, I'll come over and tell you about my trip…. Good, I'll be there about four and then stay on for dinner." She had heard the concern in her mother's voice. There would be so much to explain. She had to tell them about Joel. She would just start from the beginning and simply tell them of the abuse. She could not tell them about Alain. She longed for the comfort of her mother's arms. Her father would be another matter. Only the desire to spare his daughter public scrutiny would save Joel from his wrath.

Alain. His name had slipped into thoughts again—the same thoughts that had tormented her through the night and into this day. His face swam before her. Stop it—can't have this. Eudora caught her breath, "If I start to think about this I will cry, and I will never stop. No." Control was regained. It was still too early to begin to think about how to deal with the pain of losing him. The loss was as permanent as death and that was ironic considering he had not even yet been born. The time… how had it happened? Thoughts about that could only lead to madness.

How? How had this happened? Her mind could not begin to think of an explanation. It was an impossibility. This morning she had awakened, gotten out of bed, dressed—just an ordinary day—going about life as she had known it. All done by rote. She tried to think of traveling, tried to reconstruct her return home, but always at some point the narrative stopped. There were no logistical details in her memory and she was thrown back into the present moment where the question still lingered. *How?*

How then to deal with this? How to go on living? She could not even grieve the loss of Alain. He had existed—they had loved—how was he coping—he couldn't even know what had happened to her. How much pain was he suffering? Put this away—again. There would come a time for it, but not yet. Not yet. Her father would be able to advise her about a lawyer. Her mother would be the expert on handling social issues.

She took care of some correspondence, then spent the rest of the morning unpacking and setting things in order to prepare for the change of rooms. In the early afternoon, she sat to have tea, and noticing the time, wondered how long Joel planned to stay away. Perhaps he might even be gone overnight. What would be his counter move? She would not think about that. She planned to act, not react.

Eudora sat at her desk and looked at the list she had been making. It was her plan of escape. Steps that would be needed to free herself from the hell she refused to continue inhabiting. She thought of that hell—Joel. It was past two and he still had not returned. She turned back to her list.

She would have no need of that list.

TWO SOLEMN-FACED MISSISSIPPI STATE Troopers stood at the door. Apprehension gripped her—Mama? Daddy? Eudora invited them in then sat in disbelief as they informed her that her husband had died instantly when his car left the road on a sharp curve and went over a steep embankment before coming to rest against a tree.

She sat immobile, struck dumb.

"Mrs. Winningham, is there anything we can do for you? Is there someone we could call for you?" Both officers looked at her with concern. "Ma'am, who can I call for you?" The older officer placed a hand on her arm.

Eudora looked at him. Tears began to trickle down her cheeks. "Thank you. I can call my parents. Do you know how the accident happened?"

"We believe he must have been traveling at a high rate of speed and just couldn't make the curve."

"We'll see ourselves out, Mrs. Winningham."

She rose and thanked them, accepted a card, and promised to call if there was anything they could do. She saw them to the door, then ran upstairs to the guest room.

Devastated, she threw herself onto the bed and sobbed. When her tears were gone, the sobs were dry. She cried for possibilities that would never be made real. For love which would never be truly fulfilled. For days never to be spent together. For nights without making love. The sobs were hysterical, then quiet. Tears which had been held in check were spilled. Sorrow and loss were acknowledged. Her husband had died, but her tears and mourning were for Alain Philidor.

Unknowingly and unintended, Joel had given her a gift. She could mourn. Everyone would expect to see her mourning. They would never know the tears and sadness were not for the loss of her husband, but for a man another lifetime, another world away. She refused to feel guilty over the deception.

EUDORA WOULD HAVE PREFERRED TO let her father handle the funeral arrangements alone, but appearances would not allow that. The grieving widow had to make choices and decisions, so duties were fulfilled with her father's support. The mortuary staff provided impeccable service and guidance.

Her mother brought a suitable black dress and small veil for her to wear to the service. Joel Winningham was laid to rest in the family plot with the proper and dignified service befitting his station in life. Eudora was glad for the veil to hide the fact that there were no tears. She kept her head bowed and her hands tightly clasped in her lap.

SOUTHERN TRADITION DICTATED THAT MOURNERS be invited back to the house to express their condolences and have something to eat. Eudora's mother had supervised the staff and taken care of all of the arrangements. Eudora had to suppress the urge to smile as she looked at the table laden with food. There were various casseroles that ladies had prepared and frozen, ready to be pulled out for just such emergencies, an equal variety of congealed salads, and of course plates of deviled eggs. There was ham with Coca-Cola gravy and pineapple upside-down cakes. Only in the South would there be prescribed funeral dishes which would arrive from friends and neighbors until the crowds would be fed and the refrigerator and freezer left stocked.

The afternoon dragged on. It was difficult to hear all of the kind things said about Joel. These people did not know the monster behind the mask. Her parents had kept close to her as had Joel's.

At a moment when it was only Joel's mother hovering, she looked directly into Eudora's eyes and said, "Well, it was fortunate that you did get back from wherever it was you felt the need to go."

Eudora replied calmly, "Yes, it was. Excuse me, I need to go speak with the Reverend." The woman had lost her son. Her rudeness could be overlooked. The two women had never been close. Other than what society would dictate for public appearance, there would be no future relationship.

The last of the mourners had taken their leave. Her parents had lingered briefly, extracting a promise to call them if she needed anything. Their comforting hugs helped her to realize that this horrible day could finally be put to rest.

The staff cleaned the house of all trace of the visitors. Alone at last, Eudora sat on the veranda and sipped wine. An overhead fan stirred the cooling evening air. Cicadas were singing and the scent of jasmine filled the air.

There had been a death. There had been a funeral. There could be mourning. Mourning had to end, and life had to go on. But for now, it was okay to be sad. To cry at the hopelessness. Figuring out how life would go on could come later.

"Alain." It was breathed softly into the gathering darkness. The haunting sound of a Whippoorwill came in reply.

And life goes on—even if you think it can't—it is inevitable....

CHAPTER *16*

EUDORA DRESSED WITH CARE. TODAY would require all of the acting skills she could muster. The reading of Joel's will. She could have asked to have her parents sit in but decided against it—she had to be able to focus in one direction only—could not have the slightest distraction, even that of anyone there supporting her.

Joel's parents would be there of course. She had not seen them since the funeral. Actually, the gathering at her home afterward where Margaret had, in a manner, confronted her. Eudora took a deep breath. Would Margaret push the boundary today? If so, how would she handle Joel's mother? James had given support that might be expected of a father-in-law, yet in retrospect, it had seemed more than a little impersonal, nothing she could really count on.

Eudora closed her eyes, relaxed her shoulders, then after a quiet moment, stood and looked in the mirror. It would be all right. She looked the part of a grieving widow. Her plain black dress with a single strand of pearls presented the right picture. Her composed features barely betrayed the tears shed—tears for her real loss. *Alain.* She could not go down that road. Anytime thoughts were directed there, *How?* screamed in her mind until the screams threatened to become real and burst forth. Beyond that, there could only be oblivion.

Leaving her bedroom, she descended the stairs, picked up her keys from the hall table, and headed downtown to the impressive offices of the lawyers who handled Winningham business.

A secretary ushered her into a conference room. Herbert Tyler, the youngest partner in the firm, rose to greet her. He did not handle the bulk of the estate—the part that was still controlled by the senior Winninghams, but had worked with Joel upon his inheriting the parts of the business that had belonged to his maternal grandfather.

"Mrs. Winningham, please have a seat. May I offer you something? Coffee, perhaps?"

Eudora sat on the chair he had pulled out for her. "Coffee would be fine, thank you. Margaret. James." She acknowledged Joel's parents. James had risen when she came in. Margaret stared at her and barely nodded.

Eudora was glad that it was a round table. No choosing a side, sitting across as adversaries. She also was appreciative that the secretary promptly arrived with her coffee so that she was able to take time adding cream and sugar, then slowly stirring, giving herself a few more moments to further compose her thoughts.

Herbert Tyler looked at Joel Winningham's parents and his widow. Feeling the coldness in the room, he was glad for the contents of the document he was about to disclose. Barring any unforeseen circumstances, he did not expect any controversy.

"We are here for the reading of the last will and testament of Joel Jackson Winningham. The record will show that those present are his widow, Eudora Eugenie Campbell Winningham, and the deceased's parents, James Lee Winningham and Margaret Jane Custis Winningham." The lawyer proceeded to reveal the contents of the legal document.

Eudora was to receive the house and the property on which it was located. She also inherited ownership of several warehouses owned outright by Joel. Their rental alone would provide a generous income. Most surprising though, was the very large life insurance policy. Eudora would have been shocked if Joel had taken the policy and made her a beneficiary. Instead, when he had come into his property, he had set up a business plan and taken the insurance then, obviously having been advised to plan for the future. The insurance would go into his estate for his surviving spouse and any children. Eudora hid a smile when she thought of the irony.

His interest in the large agricultural family business reverted to his parents.

Once, while dating, Joel had driven her out to the plantation. The land was used to produce grain and raise beef cattle as well as hundreds of acres planted in cotton. This diversity kept the minerals in the soil from being depleted as so often happened when the same crop was planted year after year. A momentary cloud obstructed the sunlight and Eudora shivered as they passed one last partial standing wall of what had once been a magnificent plantation house. The cloud passed as did the troubling thought of the history of the land that now belonged to their family.

They had stopped several times to admire the fields or herds. Each time the intensity of their kisses caused Eudora to break away and insist they continue driving. Thinking back now, she thought she could recall a strange look in Joel's eyes more than once. Was there a clue there as to what he was to become—no, obviously what he was even then?

She looked at his parents. James had always been cordial and circumspect in his behavior. Warm and kind—but Joel had seemed warm and kind. Was the monster inside sired by a similar monster? Did James know what his son was? If so, did he approve, or at least condone? Was the kindly look he turned upon Eudora sincere or simply the first-generation façade?

Margaret's look was not kindly. Even at family gatherings and most intimate encounters, her warmth had always seemed superficial. Was it this coldness that nurtured the unfeeling sadist her son became? Had she denied her only child the love that would have made him a different kind of man?

Nature or nurture? Psychologists have long argued and discussed the merits of each theory. Which had produced Joel? Was it a combination, or was it neither? This was a question that would no longer claim any of her time or thought. He was past. He was dead. The hurt and wounds he had inflicted had come to an end. If only the balm that had soothed them had not left such lingering pain.

"Eudora," James's voice interrupted her thoughts. "Joel has set everything out in a very straightforward manner. The only overlap in our businesses will be the rental of the warehouses. I just want you to know that Winningham Agricultural Enterprises will continue to lease the warehouses from your estate if you agree. I will be glad to work with you or the manager you have in charge."

"Thank you, James. The current management in place has proved to be quite satisfactory. I will be meeting soon with the staff, but as things stand now, I do not anticipate any changes there. Unless you are notified of a change, you may continue to transact business with Mr. Thompson, the manager. Mr. Tyler will be my attorney of record and will handle the legal aspects of my business."

"That concludes the reading of the last will and testament of Joel Jackson Winningham." Herbert Tyler brought the meeting to a close and stood.

Leave-taking brought a hug from James but only a formal cheek-to-cheek touch from Margaret. Eudora accepted each with grace and relief. She lingered as they left the office.

"Mr. Tyler, I appreciate the way you handled this meeting. I have to admit that I was a little apprehensive as to how it would go. I'm glad that Joel did not leave any situation that would cause ill will with his parents. I hope to move forward as smoothly as possible." Eudora moved to a Queen Anne chair that Herbert had indicated near a window.

"Mrs. Winningham, I appreciate what you said about my representing your legal interests. May I draw up contracts for that association?"

"Only if you agree to call me Eudora."

"As you wish, as long as you call me Herbert." Being only a few years older, he and Eudora knew each other but had not had a social relationship.

They sat quietly as the secretary brought a new pot of coffee.

"Herbert, please do send me contracts to sign so that your firm represents my financial concerns. I will definitely take an interest in the warehouses I have inherited, but I do not want to have anything to do with their functioning. I will meet with Mr. Thompson on a regular basis and I would like for you to sit in on those meetings. I will depend on you to inform me if you find anything not going as it should. If you need a financial person added to your team to help with this, I will rely on you to choose that person." Eudora had decided that she would trust Herbert Tyler to oversee her estate. She would also keep a close eye on things herself. If managed properly, she would have a good living.

"Thank you, Eudora. It will be my pleasure to handle all of this for you."

Eudora rose and extended her hand. Herbert's firm handshake was reassuring. She felt that she had made a good start on managing her business future.

But the business at hand was to drive home—no, to the house that was now hers, but not yet home.

There is a saying, "Time heals all wounds." How much time? What to do while waiting for that time? What about now—how do I get through the next hour, the next minute, the next breath?

CHAPTER *17*

EUDORA MOURNED. SHE WAS A shadow moving through the rooms of her house. Her house, not her home. Her home was supposed to be with Alain Philidor in a beautiful country cottage near *St. Rèmy,* France.

Eudora grieved. But crying until her eyes were red could not transport her to a time and place where they would be together. That did not exist, not even in her dreams. Dreams—at least she should have had dreams of their time together, but they did not come.

The staff gave her space, not wanting to intrude, not knowing what to say to the woman who moved quietly from room to room or sat alone for hours in the garden. Her parents called daily at first, but their visits became infrequent as they realized she needed the time alone. Friends called but could not entice her to accept invitations to lunch, either out or at their homes.

Eudora existed. She had buried a husband. That chapter of her life was done and would not merit any further thought. Alain must be placed in a corner of her heart—locked safely there—he could not be a part of her future. That chapter of her life was also done but would never be gone from her thoughts, no amount of time or space could achieve that.

AUGUST 20, 2006. MY BIRTHDAY, he thought bitterly. *Thirty-one years old, and I feel one hundred and thirty-one.* He emitted a wry chuckle. How ironic—alone again.

Anna wished him happy birthday and told him she would make his favorite breakfast. He was barely able to be civil. He managed to thank her for the wishes, but declined the breakfast. He wanted to be out of the house before the phone calls began. He switched off his mobile. There would be birthday wishes from family and bandmates and he could not bear the thought of hearing their voices wish him well and inquire as to how he was doing. He could ignore voicemails or text messages if he chose. They would all be thinking of Lauren, not knowing that there was not even a small ache left for her. How could they know that somewhere past her lay an even deeper wound? A knife to the heart.

She had been gone for more than a month. She, that is how he thought of her because he could not bear to think the name. The name that had raised him to glorious heights then plunged him into deepest depths. That name and circumstances he could not begin to understand—had to stay away from thinking about them because the questions would only circle without answers—a deadly vortex to drag him down. He accepted that life had to go on. God, what a cliché!

———————

THE DREAM HAD COME AGAIN. It had not been there since the night of making love. Even in sleep, his unconscious recognized a difference. A man was standing over her but there was no violence. And the figure, which had been gradually turning, finally came into full view and Alain found himself looking into his own face. He turned back to look at the woman on the floor and reached out a hand to her, but she stood and backed away until there was only a trail of mist. He turned and walked from the stage which faded to black. The drama had played out.

When he woke, he remembered the dream but only momentarily pondered its meaning. He could not add further to the mystery, the questions, the pain of remembering his time with Eudora Winningham.

The days followed one after the other. Never differing, just being. Alain could not function. What few hours he slept were on the couch, in the living room. She had slept in both beds—it could not be there—he had tried and ended up fleeing each in turn.

What little he ate barely sustained him. He grew gaunt and hollow-eyed. He walked every day to the place where he first saw her. There was nothing left of her—and that void sucked everything from his heart and from his world.

On a gray and windy afternoon, the figure who sat among the flowers saw none of their beauty, smelled none of their perfume. Rising from among them, never to look back, the man who walked resolutely to his home was no longer bereft, but his heart was stone, his mind filled only with day to day existence—nothing left of feeling. From that moment, Alain Philidor became accomplished at going through the motions of living.

EUDORA MADE A NEW LIST. The one she had started before was to prepare for an ending—this one was to prepare for a beginning. She could not feel happy, but she felt resolved and that was a good start.

She had been surprised to find that although they had barely been married for a year, Joel had prepared that will that left so much to her. She could not even guess what had prompted his action. Guilt? Not likely. No, probably just his sense of taking care of business. Most of it had been prepared even before their marriage and he had never bothered to make changes. She was reasonably certain that he had been convinced that she would never leave him, and their marriage would play out as he chose.

The staff breathed a collective sigh of relief to hear that the estate would continue to be run as it always had. Most also had the feeling that working conditions would be more pleasant with Mrs. Winningham now in charge.

The Campbells were mildly shocked but especially pleased when their daughter called to invite them to dinner.

Eudora's last calls were made to a small group of friends from church to set up a lunch date. With satisfaction, she looked at her list and checked off the first item—reconnect with people.

The dinner with family and luncheon with friends proceeded as though there had been no interruption in their occurrence. Breeding and upbringing carried Eudora forward on a tide of false bravado. It is ironic how one can move through life's scenes so naturally that other players detect no hidden emotions, no desperate screams waiting to burst forth. Locked away in her room, she looked into her mirror, not recognizing the woman who stared back—a woman lost—a woman slowly going mad. *How?* She could not sustain the effort she had begun.

"IMOGENE, WE HAVE TO SUPPORT Eudora." Her father had seen the desperation in her eyes and heard it in her voice.

The Campbells did not understand the reason, but had quickly discerned the necessity for what their daughter was doing. She was obviously on the edge of despair. It was more than the loss of a husband—they did not pry, sensing that if it had been something, she could have shared with them, she would have. They trusted and understood when she told them that she needed to be away to think through and sort some things. They accepted the cliché as the only answer she was able to give. Perhaps there was still trauma from what she had suffered with Joel. They were heart-broken that they had not been aware of what was happening—had not been there to protect her.

Her chin quivered slightly as her mother spoke, "I know. Eudora, you will need to select hotels on your journey carefully. Have your car checked regularly at service stations. Call each evening and let us know where you are." Imogene Campbell finished the obligatory concerned motherly advice by stepping forward and clasping her daughter in a close embrace.

"I will, Mama. Thank you." She was leaving with their love, blessing, and trust.

She had a destination. St. Simon's Island, Georgia. No, that was not her destination. That was her stopping place. Her destination was... reason? Sanity? Survival? *How?*

In spite of all, love chose us—how can we let it go—how can I —how will he?

CHAPTER *18*

SHE COULD HAVE LISTENED TO the radio. Did she want to listen to music? No, any music would have brought into focus pictures that were better left unseen. Listen to news? No, there were enough conflicts in her mind, she didn't need local, national, or world crises to add to her own.

Eudora did review her travel preparations. She smiled, pleased with herself for her research, planning, and execution. The car—it was new but had been thoroughly checked by a mechanic anyway. The tires were new, and she had learned how to change one if there happened to be a flat. There were only a couple of skinned knuckles to show for the dozen practices under the tutelage of her father. Once she had looked up to see her mother standing in the window watching. Was it concern or pride on her face?

There was also the AAA card in her wallet if she found herself in need of roadside assistance. She smiled, thinking about the brochure safely tucked into the glove compartment. Imogene had highlighted every topic and phone number that she thought Eudora might need to locate quickly. Her mother was there—even when she wasn't. In spite of everything, Eudora knew that her mother's love and care were with her unconditionally.

The planned route would take her on two US highways. US 78 would get her to Columbus, Georgia, where she would spend her only night on the road, then US 82 would end at Brunswick, Georgia, where the F.J. Torras Causeway took traffic out to St. Simon's Island.

A call to the Chamber of Commerce in Columbus, Georgia, to ask for recommendations for overnight accommodations proved helpful. There were several motor courts on the list, so she had decided to look at ones when nearing the city then choose by appearance and location.

The call to St. Simon's was to a realtor. She wanted a small cottage on the shore and away from other tourists. The agent assured her that there would be a few properties from which to choose.

With packed bags stowed in the trunk of the car, she had made one final stop at her parents' home. The good-bye hugs were lingering, tears close to the surface, but unshed. Her parents would explain her absence in whatever manner seemed most logical and for the second time in six months Eudora left Booneville, Mississippi, on her own.

The day's drive was estimated to take about six hours. Eudora was so engrossed in the beauty of the scenery and peacefulness of the drive that she was surprised when she looked at her watch and found that she had been driving for two hours.

A small roadside park with a picnic table looked like a good place to pull off and stretch her legs. It was not a populated area so she would not linger, just walk for a few minutes and have some water from her thermos. The landscape was beautiful. The tall pines were interspersed with occasional magnolia trees and scores of mimosas. It must be majestic during their season of bloom. She would have liked to stay longer, but caution told her that a woman alone must be more careful, so she was on her way within ten minutes.

She burst into sudden laughter. All of this careful planning and concern about traveling alone. This from a woman who had hastily packed one suitcase and headed to France! Her laughter faded—that was when she was desperate and running for her life. And this? She returned her focus to the passing scenery.

After another two hours her stomach began to feel the need for food. As if in response to her thoughts, she spotted a diner in the distance.

The sandwich was almost finished when the waitress asked about dessert. She was about to decline when a glass case on the counter caught her eye—a case of heavenly confections! "I'll have the lemon meringue pie, please."

The words formed of their own volition. Having scraped the saucer as clean as etiquette would allow, she paid her check and was once again on the road.

The afternoon and drive were pleasant... as long as her thoughts were on the drive. There could be no thought for the reason for the trip, no thought of any other trip.

A glance at the fuel gauge let her know that there would be no need to stop for gasoline until she was ready to find a place to spend the night. Approaching Columbus, she began looking for the suggested motor courts. She passed the first two, driving slowly by and rejecting them. One did not look well kept. The bushes needed pruning and a section of fencing around the pool sagged. The second had no cars parked outside. Perhaps it was deserted for a reason. These were small things, but Eudora again realized that precautions should be taken while traveling alone.

The exterior of the third passed muster and the friendly, middle-aged woman at the desk inside asked if she would like to inspect a room. Eudora found the room to be quite clean and comfortable, so it was accepted.

The clerk was able to recommend a gas station and restaurant close by. The attendant at the service station filled the tank and checked the oil. The windshield, which looked as though it had decimated the bug population for several miles, was scrubbed clean. The small café provided a tasty light supper.

Car serviced and hunger satisfied, Eudora was safely ensconced in her room for the night. Being a newly-renovated establishment, it boasted telephones in the rooms. She called her parents and told them of the uneventful, pleasant day, relayed the information as to her accommodations, and assured them she would call the next day when she was settled into her rental.

She dressed for bed even though it was early evening. She opened the magazine she had brought for the trip but had not done much reading when her eyelids began drooping. The fresh air and almost seven hours of driving had taken their toll. After checking to make sure the alarm was set on her travel clock, she turned out the light and quickly fell asleep.

Up early the next morning, Eudora decided to drive for a while before stopping to eat. Coffee in the lobby was a welcome surprise. She paid her bill, took a cup of coffee, and began the second day of her journey.

It would be another six hours or more driving.

After an hour and a half on the road, she was definitely ready to eat. She pulled off at the first café that looked promising. She ordered ham, eggs, grits, toast, orange juice, and her second cup of coffee of the morning.

The land became flatter and the soil redder as the day wore on. Eudora thought of the charming little pinch pots made of Georgia clay. There was a row of them on a kitchen windowsill at home, each of them containing a different herb. Snippets were taken from time to time for seasoning, but the plants were allowed to grow for decoration as well. A mental note was made to look for garden pots of the same beautiful red soil.

She only made one quick stop to use the facilities but having had such a large breakfast, did not want any lunch.

The salty sea air preceded sighting of the coast, but soon signage clearly marked the way to the causeway. Filling the tank with gasoline would be a good idea since there might be fewer stations and higher prices on the island. The friendly attendant was efficient, taking little time to complete his tasks.

The causeway was a rather narrow two-lane road, but it was not heavily traveled in the middle of the afternoon as it would be later in the day when the workers left the island to return to the mainland.

The realtor had given good directions to the office so Eudora soon found it and was surprised to find the agent inside to be quite young.

"I can tell by your look you expected someone older." The young woman flashed a friendly smile. "I get that a lot."

"Not at all." Eudora recovered. "From our conversations about a rental, you seemed very well able to handle your job."

"Actually, my father owns the company." This statement was accompanied by a light, lilting laugh. "I'm Alice Brown. And of course, you are Mrs. Winningham."

"Eudora, please." Stepping forward she offered her hand. Later, she would recall the friendly gesture so quickly offered and realize that it was at that moment she ceased to be Mrs. Winningham—she did not want to be called by that name ever again. Mrs... Mrs... it *should* have been Philidor!

"My father is on his way back, so we can go ahead and head to the cottage." Alice led the way out of the office and indicated the cute little convertible they would be driving to the beach.

THE REALTOR HAD NOT EXAGGERATED when stating that the perfect rental had been found. They had passed the last house some distance back when they came to a white picket fence flanking both sides of a driveway. Little less than a quarter of a mile in the distance was the cottage. It was not large and had a slightly weathered look about it. They exited the car and walked up the two steps.

Eudora sighed, "I'll take it."

Alice laughed, "You haven't even seen the inside yet."

"Oh, I don't need to. Maybe I'll just live right here on this porch." It ran the length of the front of the house. Both the stained wood of the porch and the white walls of the house would require new coats of paint soon, as would the blue shutters at the windows, but structurally they were all in good repair. This was just a well-worn property, not neglected.

Eudora sat in one of the wooden rocking chairs, leaned back, closed her eyes, and smiled. Hearing the door open, she got up and followed Alice inside.

She forgot to breathe. Through the open door, attention was immediately drawn to the opposite side of the interior. Seen through a large window, the ocean seemed to be part of the room.

"Magnificent, isn't it?" Alice's words were an understatement.

The new tenant could only breathe, "Oh, my."

The 900-square feet of the cottage had been used to its best advantage. It had basically been divided into fourths. The first quarter to the left of the entrance was divided from the rest by walls. Through the opening into the area was a small hallway with doors leading to a tiny but efficient bathroom and a lovely little bedroom. Storage shelves with wicker baskets were located on each side of the passageway.

The back part, past the bedroom section, held a compact but fully equipped kitchen.

The other side of the interior was first a sitting room and toward the back, in front of the large window, was a small table with four chairs. A low buffet along the side wall held dishes and cutlery—no high furniture to obstruct the view.

Hearing only parts of Alice's words extolling the virtues of the cottage, Eudora drifted onto the back porch—a replica of the one on the front of the house. Sitting in one of the rocking chairs she closed her eyes and leaned back, savoring the smells and sounds.

"I apologize for my distraction. This is so unbelievably beautiful. It is absolutely perfect, Alice. There must be a high demand for this place. I must be lucky to get it."

"Actually, a lot of the tourists feel it is too far away from things. They want to be closer to the village." Alice went on to explain that was why the rental rate was so reasonable.

The young woman talked of interesting history and information about the island on the drive back to the real estate office. It was agreed that Eudora would rent for a two-week period with the option to renew for another two if the cottage were still available. Alice offered to tell her if there was another request for the property and give her the opportunity to extend before renting it to someone else.

Mr. Brown had returned to the office while they were out. He was a pleasant man in his fifties, and it was easy to see where Alice had inherited her personality. Both assured Eudora that they were there if she needed any sort of assistance.

Back in her own car, Eudora went to the market that Alice had pointed out. Driving back to the cottage, her back seat was loaded with bags. She had purchased a few staples, then found the large variety of fresh produce so seductive she filled numerous grocery sacks. She would be eating lots of fresh vegetable and fruit salads.

It took her two trips to carry in the provisions and one more for her luggage. Within an hour all the food and her belongings were put away. The call to her parents was long enough to tell them about the marvelous cottage and that the latter part of her trip had been pleasant. She gave them the phone number but also promised to call again within a few days. Necessary tasks completed, Eudora carried a plate of fruit and vegetables and the bottle of wine purchased already chilled, to the back porch.

She sat listening to the waves, the circling gulls, and the whisper of wind in the sea grass. She began eating a peach, sipped wine, and let the surroundings caress her and clear her mind. No thinking today—that would begin tomorrow. A memory almost slipped in. Another time of putting off thoughts until tomorrow.

Eudora allowed her spirit to be soothed by the last rays of the sun settling into the water and the waves lapping gently against the sand.

Alain—his kiss showed me a lifetime. He tasted of April rain, a July sunbeam, smoke from burning leaves in September and a winter snowflake caught on my tongue.

CHAPTER 19

AWAKENING WAS A MEASURED PROCESS as awareness of being co-cooned in comforting bedding pushed into her consciousness. Lying quietly, the sound of her soft breathing registered, followed by the sound of the surf. Still Eudora was reluctant to open her eyes. Having slept well, she felt well. Ready to begin her journey. She had come to think of this as a journey to reality, to sanity, to someplace safe, to the rest of her life.

Toes wiggled, a slight stretching of an arm, a full-blown arch of her body. It was time for open eyes.

The ceiling was beadboard painted white. White woodwork and pale blue walls gave the illusion of floating in a pool of light. Eudora sat up slowly. The bed was an antique iron frame that had been painted white, as had the small bedside table, armoire, and wicker chair. Everything fresh and crisp. A blue rag rug lay on the whitewashed floor.

She slid to the edge of the bed and gave a reach for the ceiling stretch before getting up and drifting toward the bathroom. There was no need to hurry into the day, nothing or no one to dictate a regimen to be followed. Her next stop was the kitchen because coffee had become a morning necessity. She smiled at the thought of her recent addiction while setting the pot to brew.

The crisp morning air that enfolded the back porch forced completion of the waking process. Arms wrapped about herself gave enough resistance to the chill to delay retreating inside. There was enough time to survey the sunlight gleaming off the sea's glassy surface, see the few gulls wheeling silently overhead, savor the salt air in her nostrils, and again realize that she was at peace, at least for the moment. With a sigh, Eudora turned slowly and went inside. Thus, began a routine that would be repeated almost daily. The first stop was the bathroom for using the facilities, brushing teeth, washing face, and running a comb through hair. Casual slacks, shirt, and canvas shoes from the armoire in the bedroom made her presentable and ready to face the day.

The crisp white linens were spread smoothly on the bed, and the quilt with the blue and yellow flowers was folded neatly across the lower half. Blue and yellow pillows were placed against the white ones she had slept on. The house was in order.

She returned to the kitchen where she prepared a plate with a toasted English muffin, an orange, and a scoop of cream cheese. She carried this along with a cup of steaming coffee to the porch and placed them on a table next to one of the rocking chairs. She picked up the cup and held it in both hands. The air was no longer quite as chilled so the long sleeves on the shirt were adequate for comfort now even though a gentle breeze had begun. As she sipped coffee and began to eat, she noticed soft musical notes from a glass wind chime at the far end of the porch. It hung from the exposed beam far enough back for protection from stronger winds. Lulled by the tinkling glass, the hypnotizing effect of the sun on the water, and the beauty of the surroundings, Eudora finished her food and drink with little awareness of passing time. The gulls, having found their own breakfast, began their bickering that jarred the observer from her reverie. She carried the dishes inside, poured another cup of coffee, and returned to the porch.

The first step to reconcile what had happened, she had decided, was to retrace her steps and look for clues. There was a huge time gap. Surely there had been something that should have been noticed as being out of place. Differences were enumerated—cars, roads, village surroundings. All had seemed only to belong to a different country, a different culture. Perhaps some things seemed different as they were considered to be catering to tourists.

Did the time difference exist only at his cottage? Had it existed in the village and escaped her notice? She didn't think so and took only a few seconds to dismiss this as something that would only bring more questions and confusion and didn't matter in the scheme of things that she had come to reconcile.

She stood and stretched, then bounded down the steps. With arms flung wide toward the sea she set off down the beach as a brisk pace.

She drew a circle in the sand with the toe of her shoe, then another circle interlocking with the first, then another and another. All intertwined, a mystery within a mystery. She reached down and picked up an object that her foot had uncovered. Turning it in her hand revealed a beautiful, unblemished little shell. Her life before Joel had been like this shell, beautiful and unblemished.

She retraced her steps and sat on the porch. She removed her shoes and dumped sand from them over the edge. Her stomach told her it was past lunch time and the clock inside confirmed it. A salad topped with cubes of ham satisfied her hunger.

A comfortable sofa was placed against the front wall of the sitting room, orientating it toward the view through the large window on the back wall. Even lying down, there was a strip of water visible beneath the expanse of sky. A table placed in front of the sofa held the little rescued shell and the novel Eudora had brought with her. She had not had a chance to read Daphne Du Maurier's latest, *My Cousin Rachel.* As though another mystery was called for! A few minutes of reading, the sun warming the interior of the cottage, the sound of the surf, and the faint tinkling of glass urged her to return the book its resting place and take the nap her body desired.

She woke with the need to move around and although it was late afternoon, she found the idea of a trip into the village appealing.

The lighthouse drew her. Situated on the southern point of the island with its brick keeper's house, it beckoned. Eudora sat on a nearby bench and stared up at the structure. Lighthouses have individual shapes and colorings so that daytime identification can help navigators pinpoint their location—this one seemed very plain, yet elegant in its simplicity.

She sat until the shadows grew long and the light flashed its beacon across the water. How far could its beam reach? Even in suspension of reality, not that far. Could anything illuminate the distance and give her just one more glimpse of his face, his smile? She chided herself for foolish thoughts as tears streamed down her cheeks. How was she to go on? Was it better to walk into the sea and sink into oblivion if going in his direction? How could she go in his direction when he did not yet exist?

Numb, with mind wiped clear of thought, she drove to the cottage, dropped her clothing on the floor, and climbed into bed.

THE JANGLING OF THE TELEPHONE in the other room jerked her awake. Jumping up in reaction and running to grab the receiver, Eudora said, "Hello."

Alice's cheerful voice came through the line. *"Eudora, this is Alice Brown."*

"Yes, hello, Alice." Her voice sounded normal as the shock of being awakened abruptly was wearing off. The clock on the wall told her that it was nine-thirty and that she had slept more than ten hours.

"I was wondering if you would like to drive in today and go to lunch. Dad is in the office and we're not expecting a busy day, so I thought you might like to have lunch and do some sightseeing."

With no hesitation she replied, "I would like that. Give me half an hour and I'll be there."

"Great, I'll see you soon then."

A quick shower, a glass of juice while drying her hair, a touch of makeup, a simple sundress, and Eudora was out the door. The melancholy of the previous evening had dissipated in the morning's hurried readying. She drove to the real-estate office looking forward to the day.

Alice came out and motioned toward her car. "I'm so glad you came."

"It was lovely of you to call." Eudora felt she was making a friend and it was a good feeling. Something that felt *normal.* Normal was good about now.

As Alice began talking, it was obvious that she was in her element. They drove northward along the coast with Alice talking about how the sunshine along with the nutrients from the area rivers soak into the marshes making them a perfect home for fish, shrimp, oysters, and crabs. Large populations of otters, raccoons, and rabbits can be found in the verdant grasslands. The coastline and dunes are protected from strong storms by these marshlands. Her narrative came to an end as she pulled up to a beautiful hotel. Though obviously having undergone restoration, it still held its original old-world authenticity and charm.

"This is the King and Prince Hotel. It opened in 1941 as a hotel but had originally opened in 1935 as a seaside dance club."

"It's absolutely magnificent." Eudora was impressed by the beauty and grandeur of the building.

"If you didn't have a big late breakfast, I thought you might like to look around a bit and then we can have an early lunch."

"I'll admit that I had been a lazy-bones this morning and only grabbed a glass of juice after you called. I'm starved."

"Then we can skip the tour and go right to lunch. I think you'll enjoy the restaurant." And there was much to enjoy. The restaurant was located in the side of the hotel overlooking the beach. The view was stunning as were the stained-glass murals in the room itself.

A white-coated waiter provided their table service and let them know that the fresh shrimp were especially nice. Both decided to have the shrimp and grits accompanied by grilled asparagus. The food was as delicious as the setting was lovely. They lingered over coffee until Alice noted the time and said that she really should go give her father a break from the office.

They chatted amicably on the short drive back. Eudora shared that she had been recently widowed and had needed to get away for a while. "I want to thank you, Alice, for inviting me today. I really enjoyed the company and the food. After all of those shrimp swimming in butter and the grits, I think I'll need to take a long walk on the beach this evening."

Both laughed and Alice replied, "I know what you mean, but every bite was worth it." They pulled into the parking lot. "Eudora, I am sorry for your loss. It must be terrible to lose your mate."

"Yes, it is," she murmured. "It truly is devastating." She was glad that Alice had not used the word *husband*. "Thank you so much again for the lovely day."

"We'll do it again soon." Alice's words were an invitation.

"Absolutely. Bye, now." Eudora pulled out of the parking space and intended to head back to the cottage, but the afternoon sun glinting off of its white shaft drew her to the lighthouse. Once again, she sat on the bench, unmoving, staring out to sea. The horizon darkened and it was not long until there were jagged streaks of lightning in the distance. She gathered herself and drove directly to the cottage. She pulled the car close to the side of the building and wished there had been a garage.

Inside, she called her parents to reassure them again that she was safe and doing well. The latter was not quite the truth, but there was no need to add worrying her parents to her list of dilemmas.

Carrying the remains of last night's bottle of wine, the back porch was once again her evening destination. The storm clouds were coming near land and the wind had picked up. The glass pieces of the wind chime danced to their own music. Streaks of lightning rent the sky with the following thunder drowning out the sound of the surf.

The storm within once again raged, echoing the conflagration over the sea. Questions louder than the distant thunder pounded inside her head. Why? To have found such a love and then it be denied—and denied in such a bizarre and final way. She could not even tell of her love—could not share the joy of finding love—could only keep her own counsel. Had it even been real? It *had* to have been real. This much pain could only have been born of reality. And the ever present, *How?* Always there in the back of her mind, ready to spring into tortuous thought.

The fury of the storm abated before it made landfall, but rain began drifting down in sheets. The wind carried it onto the porch, but still the solitary figure did not move to go indoors. It was impossible to separate the raindrops from the tears cascading down her face. Presently she rose and walked down the steps toward the water. Face lifted to the heavens, her voice was beseeching, "Alain! Alain!" The gale hurled the words back at her. With her head hanging low and shoulders sagging, she walked back inside.

From ancient times, men have gone to sea while women have stood on jagged cliffs or sandy shores waiting and watching. But they had hope....

CHAPTER 20

THE SMELL OF RECENT RAIN and sea salt mingled in the first moments of awakening. Her first thought was what a lovely experience it was to wake here. Slowly, object by object, becoming aware of pleasant surroundings. Stretching then burrowing under covers was a luxury that could become habit.

A soft rain began pattering against the window, rain so opposite to last night's storm. She pushed the memory aside and fell back into restful sleep.

The sun was well up when she opened her eyes again—no more indulging herself—sitting on the side of the bed for only a moment, she was up. Wet clothes that had been hurriedly dropped on the shower floor last night were wrung out and laid in the sink to be added to a load of laundry in the small washing machine.

Speed of motion reduced the need for thinking outside the task at hand. Shower, dress, laundry, cereal, fruit, coffee on the table. Ensconced in the adjacent rocking chair—calming sea, shoulders relaxed, soothing of spirit.

As the storm had cleansed the beach of debris, screaming into the wind had vented her rage and cleared debris from her mind. At that moment came the realization that her rage had been against him. Why could he have not been able to do something to keep her? That was unreasonable, of course. He did not know. If he had, he would have moved heaven and earth to keep her with him. How could rage be directed against fate, an intangible? Perhaps one hurdle had been cleared.

THE LIGHTHOUSE DREW HER—FOR no apparent reason. Looking up at it seemed to offer something, but gave no inkling as to what that might be. It was a pleasant place to sit, a place of belonging. There was more than the flashing warning light here, there was history. In a park across the way, live oaks reached moss draped arms and gnarled fingers toward the earth below their spreading heights. What panorama of living had they witnessed through time? Did years pile upon themselves in a jumble of no particular order? It was the how of the years that haunted her. It was the question with no answer. How had time been different? How? was the initiator of madness. The ever-present question.

Eudora returned to the cottage where she sat on the porch and looked at the sea. Her days fell into this pattern. She called Alice to renew her stay at the cottage for another two weeks. She felt a little guilty due to not answering the phone a few times earlier, telling Alice that she must have been on the beach. The truth was that she had wished for solitude, but now she had an appointment with the promise of an island tour.

ALICE HAD PACKED A LUNCH to be shared along the way. The stop was at a shaded picnic table by the beach road. Looking toward the marshy area along the shore, Eudora remembered another picnic in a similar location but far, far away. The thundering of hooves clouded in rolling mist, then the magnificent horses coming into view. It had been a day of magic, a day of love, riding through the rain, staying at his house. If only he had come into her room that night, they could have shared another night of love—maybe they would have discovered the anomaly and some solution could have been found. If only….

"Earth to Eudora…." Alice's voice called her back to the present.

"I am so sorry. I was engrossed in the beauty of this place." Even as she spoke, a pod of dolphins began a display close to the shore. They commanded the attention of the watchers who ate in silence. The animals moved on, lunch was finished and remains packed up.

"Well, I have to warn you that I spent two summers giving guided tours of the island so if I start boring you, just let me know." Alice began her narrative as she pulled the car onto the road. "What we are approaching is Fort Frederica National Monument, which was established in 1936. The fort was the military headquarters of Georgia during the early colonial period. It was important because of the Spanish in Florida. The Spanish were ousted from this area in 1742 after the British won the Battle of Bloody Marsh. That was the end of the War of Jenkin's Ear."

Eudora snapped her head around to look at the narrator. "The war of *what?*"

Alice smiled, showing that this was the usual response to that statement. "The War of Jenkin's Ear. The story goes that the Spanish Coast Guard had cut off the ear of one, Captain Robert Jenkins in 1731. When the captain was asked to testify to Parliament in London, he supposedly displayed his severed ear as evidence."

"Eew," accompanied by wide eyes and scrunched up nose.

"Exactly! But the English ambushed the Spanish, who were marching single file, thus the victory at Bloody Marsh."

"Well, your history certainly is colorful." Eudora could not resist the pun.

Alice laughed and acknowledged Eudora's sense of the ridiculous. They ambled through the historic area looking at the displays for the better part of an hour and then moved on. Not far up the road, an ancient church came into view. A metal placard announced that it was Christ Episcopal Church.

Alice began, "The first church was built in 1820 but it was damaged by Union troops during the War of Northern Aggression." Both women smiled at this. "This structure was built in 1884 and is still an active church."

"Lovely," Eudora breathed quietly. There was a stillness, a serenity, a calm about the place and she felt it.

They walked among the gravestones in the cemetery. Alice pointed out that the oldest was from 1803. There was a feeling of sadness while looking at the stones marking graves of local youth who had fallen during the Civil War. Eudora was surprised to see the graves of Union troops close by.

"The Wesley brothers, Charles and John, were important figures in early religious activities here. Along with a Reverend George Whitfield, they ministered to the colonists of Fort Frederica. John returned to Europe and is considered to be the father of Methodism. Charles is known for writing hymns. Would you like to go inside the church?"

"Yes, I would." Eudora walked ahead of her guide. The interior was dark wood patterned with colors created by light streaming through the stained-glass windows. She sat on a pew in silence, as she had in St. Martin, trying to decide her future. What futility! Not even aware that the choice would not be hers to make. She wanted to scream. She wanted an *answer.* Religion had not been a close personal relationship for her, but now, once again, she prayed in silence, "Oh, God, how? Why? I love him so."

Love him so. That was the crux of it.

A love that had no possibilities.

She turned a calm face toward Alice, who, perhaps sensing Eudora's need for solitude, had moved to the back of the sanctuary. "It's a beautiful place, Alice. A comforting place."

"It is. I have sometimes come here just to sit and think if I had a problem or some decision to make. I seem to find solace here."

The women walked into the bright sunshine, then began their journey back to the office. "Oh, I forgot to tell you, there will be a quiz to see if you remember all of the dates I threw at you." Alice laughed. "I just find it helps to sort of keep time in perspective to include them."

"It certainly does." Time perspective—dates—are they real? A number flashed before her eyes. *2006.* Real? Again, *how* hammered in her brain.

After leaving Alice, Eudora drove by the lighthouse but did not stop.

She carried a plate of light supper and took up her nightly vigil watching the sea.

———————

SHE WAS HERE AGAIN. SHE had spent many hours here, sometimes staring out to sea, but often staring up at the light.

"The lighthouse is said to have a ghost. Sorry, I didn't mean to frighten you. I've noticed that you seem to have a particular interest in my lighthouse."

Oblivious to the man's approach, Eudora had jumped, startled by his words. *"Your* lighthouse?"

"Yes, I'm the keeper here."

"It is an interesting structure. I've enjoyed just sitting here looking at it and the ocean." And she had been drawn to come here once again.

"Would you like to see the light?"

She hesitated, but since there were other people in the area, she decided that he couldn't very well be an axe murderer taking her inside the building to hack her to pieces.

"I would, thank you." Introductions were made, but small talk soon abandoned as the 129 steps of the spiral iron staircase required most of their lung capacity. Once at the top and looking at the light, Eudora nodded and looked interested in his narrative about the structure, the light, types of lenses, but her gaze wandered to the water—seen from this height it seemed to stretch on forever. Forever—that was the distance to where he was—forever.

"You mentioned a ghost?" Definitely more interesting than asking a technical question.

"The ghost is said to be that of Frederick Osborne, a keeper who was killed in a duel with his assistant. There were conflicting stories as to the reason for the duel. One was that Osborne constantly found fault with the assistant's work. Another purported that the assistant had made an unwanted advance to Osborne's wife. Whatever the cause, Osborne had a pistol, but armed with a shotgun, the assistant fatally wounded the keeper."

"What happened to the assistant?"

"Acquitted of all charges. So, Osborne just hangs around—looking for justice, maybe. Or maybe just to annoy the keeper," this accompanied by a wide grin.

"And what about you? Have you met the ghostly Mr. Osborne?" Her tone was light and slightly teasing.

"Nope, the old boy seems to have left the premises totally in my care." This time he offered a hearty laugh. After the descent, Eudora thanked the keeper again and walked toward her car. She turned to look at the lighthouse one last time. Another door had closed. The view from the top brought her no closer to an answer. She did not even realize that she had been searching locations for the answer—*how?* The answer was not to be found in a location, a person, anywhere. It was not to be found because it did not *exist.*

She sat in her usual evening spot on the porch. The sun setting behind her sent shafts of light across the water beyond the point shaded by objects on the land. Eudora leaned back in the chair and closed her eyes. Waves lapped, glass tinkled, and a lone gull cried plaintively. She reflected on her experiences since coming to the island. She admitted now that it had not been just a matter of getting away. She had known that before, now that was internalized. It had been a journey of discovery—or hoping to make a discovery. An explanation. And the explanation was that there was none.

She retraced every detail of her time with Alain. A gust of wind blew across the porch. She was jarred from her lassitude as though hit by a thunderbolt. What a disservice she was doing to Alain, to the memory of what they had! They had hours when they should have had years, but had they known those hours were all they were to have, they could not have made them count for more. They were perfect hours of loving, not tainted by an impending end. This continued languishing in agony diminished the beauty of what had been. She quieted in body and mind. Her breathing became deep and even. Her hands lay quietly in her lap. Thoughts ceased swirling in maddening circles. Slowly and deliberately she rose from her chair and gave a final look around.

She walked inside and resolutely picked up the phone and dialed. When the voice on the other end answered, she said, "Mama, I'm coming home. I'll be staying tomorrow night at the same place I stayed on the way here."

Ready for an item on the list she had made weeks ago, she picked up a beautiful book bound in red leather. Begun in France, her journal must be continued before memory could fade and details lost. Every moment must be recorded and kept. She was glad she had brought this with her.

The writing was therapy. As pages filled, moments were relived, and acceptance began. Reality had to be accepted, the reality that those few weeks in a future time had existed. In accepting that, she also accepted that there was no point in trying to understand how that had happened. The time spent with him was *real*. His kisses and his touch were *real*. Making love with him was *real*.

The second reality to be accepted was that no matter how real that time was, it was gone, and it had no connection to the present or the future. There was that disconnect to be dealt with. Her last memory there was of making a decision to remain with Alain. She remembered taking off her wedding ring and throwing it into the darkness of the garden. The wedding ring that was not on her finger when she returned home.

Her next memory would be that of being in the taxi that delivered her home in a confused and dazed state. She had gathered herself enough to just keep putting one foot in front of the other and not to think of anything but that next step.

A disconnect of time—the phrase was written—not to be questioned or agonized over again.

SHE PACKED, TIDIED THE COTTAGE, wrote a long note to Alice then sealed it in an envelope with the key. She would put it in the office drop box early in the morning as she left the island.

It felt good to climb into the bed. Physically and emotionally exhausted, but resolute, she was soon asleep.

She was aware of sleeping on her side with knees pulled toward her chest. There was the warmth of a body close to hers, curling around her—an arm reaching around and pulling her into the warm circle, lips brushing her neck. "Alain," she sighed.

EUDORA AWOKE REFRESHED EARLY THE next morning. As she had planned, she was on her way when the sun was barely above the horizon. She was going home.

I sat to write, thinking of this as an anniversary, and it is—the anniversary of the beginning of the rest of my life. It is a year since I returned from France. It was not the anniversary I wished to recall—that is the hours, the minutes, I spent with Alain Philidor. I was blessed to have been able to draw Alain just as I remembered him from that day. In memorializing his face, I have done all of which I am capable to never forget my time with him. Never forget that we loved.

CHAPTER *21*

WINTER FOLLOWED AUTUMN AND WAS in turn supplanted by spring then summer again. Budding trees burst into full blown foliage. Eudora sat on the veranda. Evening sounds filled the air, and blossoms on the magnolia tree perfumed the summer breeze. Thoughts successfully locked away most hours nudged their way through. One year ago, today. One year. She had stepped from the taxi in a state of shock and bewilderment to begin life over.

In that year she finished her official time of mourning. She smiled at that thought because a year designated for mourning was such a conventional thing. She had broken convention when she fell in love with Alain. But Southern traditions were still important to her, and she was proud of being a Southern woman. Realizing that had been a comfort to her and with it had come the knowledge that valued traditions did not impose limits but rather voluntary boundaries that gave a comforting structure.

Eudora had come to know herself. Many hours spent in evaluation of her life, her values, had led to a blueprint for the framework in which she wanted to live her life. The details of living would come at their own times, but the foundation on which to build the rest was firmly in place.

The hum of a mosquito let her know that it was time to go inside. She walked through the entry hall and up the stairs where she paused to look back. Looking at parts of the refurbished living room and dining room brought a smile to her lips. Continuing on to the master bedroom she walked into the redecorated space—her room, in her home. And in reality, it had finally become her home. Life settled into a pattern—not boredom, just a comfortable and comforting pattern.

———————

THE FIRST BAPTIST CHURCH OF Booneville, Mississippi, was established in 1868. Eudora's ancestors could be traced back to that beginning. Now Eudora attended services regularly. Her experiences in St. Martin and Christ Episcopal Church had planted seeds that took root and grew into a spiritual awakening which brought peace and calmness into her life. It was balm to the pain—a relief but never a complete healing. She was reminded by the scriptures that we are not to question God. She did not ask "Why?" quite so often now. But at times when the pastor spoke of the beauty that God had created on earth, she could not keep a vision of flower filled fields in Provence from coming into focus.

When hymns were soft and poignant, a voice slipped unbidden from her heart into her ear.

———————

THE COOK WOULD BE PLEASANTLY surprised when she saw the kitchen was as clean as she had left it. Eudora had decided that she was doing the baking herself. The church ladies' group was having a bake sale to provide funds to help stock the local food pantry as there would be a higher need with the coming season. The pecan tassies and sweet potato pies cooling on the racks received proud glances as the baker restored the counters to the pristine condition in which she found them. Beautifully tempting items baked with care in a Southern kitchen. She couldn't help thinking that they should have been baked with love in the quaint kitchen of a French cottage.

Carefully sealed into containers and ensconced on the back seat of her car, the sweets were transported into town. Several civic groups participated in the food drive, so it had turned into quite an event. Canopies set up in the town park housed different groups who were already manning their stations with homemade treasures and mouthwatering treats.

She drove past the Elks Club booth which had stolen the show the past several years with a demonstration in front of their tent. A huge iron kettle hung over a fire pit. A club member was kept busy continuously stirring the contents with a long wooden paddle. Wafting from the kettle was the smell of apples, cinnamon and the secret ingredient. It drew everyone in the vicinity to their area sooner or later. One gentleman, with an old-fashioned dipper, would ladle small amounts into tiny cups for onlookers to sample. The recipient would blow on the steaming offering, tentatively taste, finish every drop, then immediately buy at least one jar from the stock of Ball-pint jars lining the shelves at the back of the tent. As the fame of their apple butter spread, the members and their wives increased the stock every year. Eudora was pretty sure that the secret ingredient was a dash of rum. She smiled at the thought of seriously devout citizens, who would staunchly stand against the demon rum, buying the apple butter that would top many buttermilk biscuits.

She reached the Baptist Ladies' booth, unloaded her containers, modestly accepted the praise extended, and set about organizing the items for sale. A plate of small pastries caught her eye—she had seen ones like that before—shared at a picnic lunch—a finger wiping a dab of cream from the corner of her mouth, then twinkling eyes staring into hers as he enjoyed the taste of the cream and the vision of her smile.

SINCE 1901 THE JUNIOR LEAGUE has represented Volunteerism with a capital V. Eudora's grandmother had been a charter member in Booneville. Miss Imogene had served in the local organization as chair of various committees and through the rank of offices until becoming president. Eudora had no choice—she was a member of Junior League. This was one instance where her mother might have been unable to conceal her disappointment had Eudora not followed tradition.

Eudora would have chosen the membership anyway. The organization's dedication to building leadership skills and character and providing community service gave her a sense of purpose that was vital to her survival. Her life had to count for something. Her involuntary sacrifice had to matter.

The projects to raise money were imaginative and fun. Each one in turn became her favorite, but forced to choose, she would have chosen the Christmas bazaar. The booth was always decorated with garlands of magnolia leaves and pine boughs, the latter giving off an air that drew focus to the season and its meaning. There were the usual baked goods, but also a wide variety of handcrafted items.

Eudora had given a lot of thought to what she might produce, then one day, looking through a catalog that offered a wider variety of items than usually found in such publications, she saw an offer for imported French lavender. Her mind said, "No," but her fingers moved under different direction and placed the order. She purchased lavender colored organdy and sewed small bags to be filled with the herb, then tied them with narrow purple satin ribbon. As she worked, she remembered. The memories were no longer so painful, more a sweet sorrow. There came a day Eudora decided that remembering had become wallowing, so she stored the sachets in an unused guest room. More than once, in the middle of the night, she found herself standing outside the door of the room. Some nights she went in. Some nights she didn't.

———

"EUDORA, IT'S A GOOD THING the bazaar is held in such a large space. This lavender would overpower everything in a smaller area. It may even rival the pine boughs in the hall." Smiling proudly, Imogene looked at the large box on the back seat of the car.

"Well, Mama, I have left the window open in the guest room, but it may have to stay open for a week!" The women laughed together, the daughter thankful for a mother who gave her unconditional love and support, the mother who saw evidence that the daughter she loved with all her heart was returning to the happy girl she had raised—no, a girl no longer, but a happy and confident young woman.

EUDORA HAD BEGUN TO LOOK forward to the short trips to Oxford. When asked to serve on the board of Kappa Kappa Gamma at Old Miss, she was hesitant but eventually agreed. It was quickly discovered that her talents lay in overseeing upkeep of the house. Under her supervision, major repairs were undertaken. Donations poured in from alumni and parents of current students that allowed for updating the interior. Working with a committee of residents, a coordinating theme was planned for highly anticipated redecorating.

The girls gave no end of suggestions, and Eudora incorporated many of them into her final plans for the common areas. There were three basic designs from which to choose for the individual rooms and the sisters had leeway to pick, then add their own personal touches to their private space.

It was on her way home after a trip to Oxford that Eudora suddenly realized that she was truly happy in the life she was leading. It might be a day-to-day happiness, but with it came a feeling of security and a sense that at least for a while she could safely remember that brief life, the life where she knew love, knew bliss, knew Alain Philidor.

"SUSAN, IF YOU'RE FREE TOMORROW afternoon at three, I would love to meet you at the country club for tennis. I know I'm terribly out of practice, but I promise to try to at least make the match interesting." She could almost hear the surprise at the other end of the line, but her old tennis partner enthusiastically accepted the invitation. Eudora smiled. Another facet of her life to renew—the country club.

The tennis date was a success. Her entry back into the activities of that group was the topic of conversations and several phone calls for the next few days until there was more current news for gossip. There were numerous club activities in which to participate and functions to attend—but only those that did not require an escort—that door remained closed—behind that door there was only loss.

A friend said, "Someday you will find someone special again." I began to believe....

CHAPTER 22

EUDORA HUNG UP THE PHONE and laughed aloud. She didn't know who was in the bigger tizzy, her mother, or her friends. The telephone would ring several times a day with some form of the same question. Did she know about the new man in town? Has she noticed him in church? Isn't he the most handsome thing? Has she seen that precious little sporty convertible he drives? Does she know he has taken one of the lovely apartments in Mrs. Farmington's building?

Eudora could just hear the wheels turning in their heads. The invitations would start soon. *"Eudora, we are giving a small dinner party for the new president of the bank and I would be ever so grateful if you would come to make my table even numbered."* What an interesting way to put it!

"Eudora, darling, your father and I are having a small cocktail party to introduce the new bank president to a few of our friends. You will come, won't you?" That was as subtle as her mother was capable of being.

"Eudora, our Sunday school class is planning a picnic. Do you think you might invite that new bank president?"

Did none of them know his name or was he going to be forever referred to as the new bank president? Eudora smiled. The smile grew wider as she realized this was the first thing that had amused her in a long time—too long—but she did not accept any of the invitations.

"EUDORA, IT IS TIME YOU met Cameron Mason." Imogene Campbell had nudged her daughter into a turn. They had just descended the church steps and Eudora, walking ahead of her mother, had headed toward the parking lot.

She paused and smiled, knowing she was going to be facing the new bank president when she turned. Steel gray eyes looked into hers. A twinkle warmed them.

"The New Bank President," Eudora said with a hint of mischief as she extended her hand.

As he accepted her proffered greeting, the man momentarily looked puzzled, then laughed. "Well, I understand that I have been described in that manner quite a lot since my arrival in town. Hello, Mrs. Winningham."

"Please, call me Eudora." She had repeated this as often as possible without creating curiosity—she could not bear that name. She might never be completely free of it, but she did not want to hear it any more than necessary.

"Then you must call me Cameron or call me by my initials, TNBP." The twinkle in his eyes deepened as it was Eudora's turn to laugh. He continued, "It is a pleasure to finally meet you. I have seen you a few times at a distance and at church, but have always just missed an introduction."

"Are you enjoying your new city?" Eudora was finding it easy to talk with the newcomer and was almost reluctant to go when her mother reminded her that they were meeting her father who was returning from a business trip.

"I am, but I would love to learn more from a native. May I call you?"

Had she actually been concerned that he might not ask? "I would like that. I don't have a pen to write my number, but I'm in the phone book."

"I know." She saw him smile as he walked away.

The drive to the airport would take about an hour as the nearest one servicing Booneville was located in Tupelo. They were fortunate that this airport had recently started handling limited passenger service. She remembered the ride in the hired car when she had fled, worried that somehow, he would find her before she could board a plane. She remembered nothing of the return trip.

Imogene did not break the silence in the car as they rode toward the airport. Eudora was lost in her own thoughts. Conflicting ones tried to force their way into her head, but she successfully controlled them and allowed only the ones dealing with the present. *Here and now.* It was becoming her mantra. I am here. This is now.

"You know, he seems very pleasant."

Imogene jumped at the sound of her daughter's voice. "He is quite pleasant. He is witty and quite knowledgeable on a wide range of subjects. He is the dream of every mother with a daughter of marriageable age in this town. Although never having been married, he is considered beyond the age for coming out parties, which seems to be a relief to him. I have heard more than one lady sigh, 'If only he were a bit younger,' while the daughter held the opinion that while he might be a little too old for a debut, he was the perfect age for husband material."

The topic of Cameron Mason was dropped when they reached the airport. They arrived at the gate just in time to greet Jefferson Campbell. The ride home was filled with news of his trip and their activities while he had been away. They made one stop to have a light lunch.

"Eudora has finally met Cameron Mason." Imogene could not keep the pleasure from her voice.

"And what is the verdict, honey?" Jefferson's question was directed to his daughter.

"He seems quite nice."

"Well, that's not exactly high praise, now is it?" Her father laughed at her noncommittal reply.

"Okay, he seemed very nice and he is going to call me." The three of them laughed together—a laugh that said it felt good—to all of them.

THE MAN WHO STOOD TO greet her was well put together. Neatly creased khaki slacks, open neck shirt, navy blazer on his six-foot frame, chestnut hair well brushed, a broad smile of welcome as he held the chair for her to sit. He had waited a week before calling her, and then it was to suggest that if she happened to be coming into town anytime soon, they should meet for coffee. The man could not be accused of moving too quickly.

They ordered coffees, and finding the wonderful looking tea cakes in the display case irresistible, indulged and declared them worth every bit of sugar involved.

Their conversation was light and amiable with Eudora giving interesting moments of history of the area and her family, which Cameron was eager to hear. The talk drifted to a more somber note when he began to speak of his family. He was born and raised in Natchez, an only child. Both of his parents were deceased—both lost to heart disease.

"That's why you won't find me giving in to these tempting sweets very often. Since there are heart problems on both sides of my family, I try to stick to a healthy diet and exercise regularly."

Eudora reached over and put her hand on his. "I am so very sorry about your family," she said quietly.

"Thank you. Now tell me about this social season. I know we had all of the debutant balls back in Natchez. When I was the appropriate age, I was invited to all of them. I truly enjoyed the parties, but I had the feeling that I barely escaped the plans of some of the mothers." He laughed.

His comments mirrored what her mother had told her earlier about the current circumstances. Some traditions would never change.

"Thank goodness I am definitely too long in the tooth to be included in all of that here." They laughed—particularly at the idea that they were somehow past the age for what now seemed so frivolous.

"I have to admit that I did enjoy my coming out season—all of the balls and parties." A shadow erased her smile. "I met my husband at my ball."

The waitress refilling their coffee was a welcome interruption to the conversation.

Cameron spoke as soon as she had left. "I think we have known each other long enough now that it would not be improper for me to ask you on a real date. Will you have dinner with me Saturday night?"

"I would love to," the quickness of her response surprised both of them.

They agreed on a time for him to call for her. She scooted her chair back, so he quickly rose and pulled it away for her to stand. "I've enjoyed our conversation very much, Cameron."

"So have I, Eudora."

She liked the way his voice sounded when he said her name. It was a good beginning.

———————————

SINCE THEY HAD NOT DISCUSSED where the dinner date would take place, Eudora was in a quandary as to what to wear. She decided on a simple navy-blue dress and pearls—pearls were always good. She smiled at the fact she was interested in such a small detail.

Her parents had been visiting since the afternoon, her father going over some of the business records she had asked his advice about. When she heard the doorbell, she knew her parents would answer it, but found herself eager to greet her date, so hurried out of her room.

Cameron had arrived precisely on time. Eudora saw the pleasure in his eyes as he watched her descend the stairs. She saw the glow on her parents' faces as they looked from one to the other. Thinking about the significance of this should have been disquieting, but it wasn't. Life was easy, the need to guard thoughts seemed to be passing away.

They drove to a small country inn that had a reputation for having the most talented chef in the county, and he did not disappoint. They ordered the dishes enthusiastically recommended by their waiter and were rewarded with a culinary masterpiece. They did skip dessert, but lingered over coffee.

"I would like to visit Natchez for the spring or fall pilgrimage sometime." Eudora referred to the events where beautiful gardens and magnificent old homes were showcased and opened to the public for special tours.

"It is a spectacular time," Cameron replied, "The garden clubs sponsor the festivities. A large number of private homes are opened for the tours and special evening events are included also. It all ends with a magnificent tableau portraying the history of the city."

"I've heard a few interesting stories and high praise from friends who have been there for the events. One interesting story was about how the pilgrimages got started. The gardens had been a large tourist draw for quite some time, but frost got them one year. Supposedly, in order to not lose the tourist revenue, one of the women said, 'Ladies, get out your mamas' wedding gowns, put them on, and give tours of your homes,' and the pilgrimages were born."

"That sounds pretty accurate, I think. There are several of those ladies still living and active in the garden club. Mother has always spoken admiringly of the founders."

"I also heard stories about rival garden clubs—someone couldn't get into the original so started their own, which attracted quite a few members."

"Mother never really mentioned any rivalry but did say that the pilgrimage became a cooperative effort of the two groups." He laughed, "I do remember mother talking about negotiations for sharing the spotlight as royalty at the tableau."

Realizing they were almost the last people in the restaurant, they rose to leave. The hostess smiled, saying she hoped they had enjoyed their evening and would return. Both assured her that they would. They grinned at each other, having spoken at the same time, and saying almost exactly the same words. It had been a good evening.

The drive to her home was not long. They were relatively quiet, only a few small talk comments.

Cameron pulled the car to a stop in the circular drive in front of the house, got out, walked around, and opened her door. As she stepped out and looked up, their eyes met. He took her elbow and guided her up the steps. When they reached the door, he clasped her hand. His touch felt good, but Eudora found herself becoming tense.

"It was wonderful to spend time with you, Eudora. Thank you. May I call you again?"

"I would like that—very much—thank you."

He gave her hand a gentle squeeze then opened the door for her to go inside.

She stood leaning back against the door for a few moments before ascending the stairs to her bedroom. Once there, she was in a hurry to get into bed and lie quietly with her thoughts which were anything but quiet. Were her heart and head again to be in conflict?

It did not take a crystal ball to tell her that there was more to come with Cameron Mason. When she passed into that realm of thought, feelings of disloyalty accompanied them. Alain, and with that name, still a tear. But the voice of reason told her that he was not real. "But he was real," she countered, "but not now, and I am living now." In the middle of these conflicted thoughts, the phone beside her bed rang.

"I just wanted to call to wish you goodnight again." Cameron's voice was soft and caring.

"Thank you and goodnight."

His final, *"Goodnight,"* came through the phone, and she held it seconds more before replacing the receiver.

So many times, she had resolved to move on. This time if that resolve could be kept, she believed for the first time that there was a destination, a place to live her life. Could emotion and sensibility finally unite without fear of the outcome?

The beauty of this day was reflected in his eyes when he looked into mine and took my hand in his. I would be Cameron's wife....

CHAPTER 23

EUDORA HAD AWAKENED EARLY AND sat on the veranda watching morning lazily bloom into full sunlight. She ran through a list of final preparations in her head. Tomorrow would be her wedding day. She had come to love Cameron Mason very much. Wanted a life with him, a *family*. This realization had come through time spent together. Time he had given her to learn that she could love without fear. She had escaped the fear of the treatment she had received from Joel. She had dealt with the pain of her involvement with Alain. She had no fear in her love for Cameron.

She lingered, sipping coffee, listening to the birds, savoring the new day. A smile curled her lips as she remembered Cameron's proposal. It had been a morning like this. While sitting in this very spot, she was surprised to hear a vehicle tearing up the driveway. She could see that it was Cameron's car and was frightened that something terrible had happened to have him coming this early in the day, without calling, driving like a crazy person.

She barely had time to get up from her chair before he came rushing toward her.

"Marry me! You have to say you will marry me!" He had dropped to one knee in front of her.

Eudora clutched her hands to her chest. "Wh... what?"

"Marry me."

He had not moved. Eudora looked down at him, stunned into silence.

She found her voice. "Cameron Mason, you just scared the life out of me! Have you completely taken leave of your senses?"

"Yes, I have! I have just spent a sleepless night thinking of all sorts of romantic scenarios about how to propose to you. The sun was coming up, and I thought, "To hell with this! I just have to go ask the woman. I love you, Eudora, and I can't imagine my life without you." He looked up with a pleading, boyish smile. "What more do I have to say before you say yes and let me get up from here while my knees are still willing. I think my left leg is going to sleep!"

"Get up from there." A small giggle escaped but was quickly followed by a shy smile. "Of course, I'll marry you," she whispered.

Cameron jumped to his feet, swooped her up and swung her around. They collapsed against each other in laughter.

"What on earth has gotten into you?" She caught her breath and looked into his eyes. What was reflected there was the life they were to share. She leaned her head against his chest and listened to the heartbeat that was her lifeline.

"I've always been conservative, restrained, but I knew this was the time for throwing caution to the wind. I couldn't take a chance that you would think that I'm just a boring banker."

They dissolved once more into laughter.

———————————

THEIR KISSES HAD BEEN LONG and tender. The method had been a surprise, but Eudora had known the proposal was coming. She had thought long and hard and searched her soul—and her heart.

She would never forget Alain. He would always have a place in her heart, but she also loved Cameron. He was the present. He was reality. She knew he would ask her to marry him and that in order to accept, she had to be sure that she was not cheating him of anything a man had a right to expect from his wife. She was sure, and on that glorious morning with its unexpected turn of events, her course was set to become Mrs. Cameron Mason.

This wedding would be so different from the one before. First would be a small ceremony in the family church, then a reception at their home. It could be called their home because after the proposal, she and Cameron began to plan their future. The first thing to consider was where they would live. He loved her home and there were no ghosts there for her. Her extensive renovation of the house had made it completely free of any trace of the horror that had inhabited it. The proper plans and documents had been drawn up to ensure this was a place where they could build a future.

They were to honeymoon in Italy. Eudora had asked if they might do that as Cameron definitely wanted to go to Europe and she could not take the chance that he would suggest France. She could never go to France....

———————————

"IT IS EXACTLY LIKE A MOVIE! I've seen this very moment a dozen times." Eudora was amazed as she was handed into the gondola by Cameron. The gondolier pushed away from the steps and onto the smooth water into the Venetian night.

The new husband pulled the new bride close and kissed her as the boatman began to sing. The evening was every cliché ever voiced or envisioned about the canal ride in Venice—cliché, yet completely new because it was their first time.

The boatman proved an entertaining guide, pointing out the Rialto Bridge and other well-known landmarks, as well as the not so well-known, which made the evening more interesting.

Too soon the enchanting ride ended. Or maybe not too soon. They were delivered back to the Hotel Gritti Palace where they were to spend their first night in Italy. They found the staff had unpacked their luggage into the lavish Venetian suite.

Cameron sat, then pulled Eudora down onto the couch beside him. She rubbed her hand over the rich blue brocade and looked up at him.

"Thank you. You have chosen the most absolutely beautiful place in the world for our honeymoon." She looked around the room—two antique chairs were covered in the same fabric. The skirt around the bed was a darker hue, banded in gold, while the coverlet was snow white. Floor to ceiling draperies matched the bed skirt. A rug that was obviously an antique covered the middle of the ancient floorboards. Painted walls were ivory with ample gilding on moldings. The lighting fixtures were unmistakably Murano glass.

"I couldn't bring you anywhere other than a perfect setting." His eyes adored her as his fingers began to work with the buttons on her sweater.

The turndown service had included scattering rose petals on the pillows. He lifted her onto the bed.

Eudora looked up into the eyes of the man who was her husband. She saw the knight in shining armor—she saw the happily ever-after—she saw the future she had first envisioned when she had accepted his proposal. He slowly finished undressing her, then stood and just as slowly removed his own clothing. She held up her arms to him and sighed softly as he covered her body with his.

She was sure that Cameron had been completely open with her about his past which had contained only one serious relationship and that had ended by mutual consent. There were no demons to haunt him.

They had made love and lay locked in an embrace. Cameron had drifted off to sleep but Eudora could not still her mind enough for sleep to come. She moved quietly, but almost immediately he was awake. In the moonlight she could see the concerned look on his face.

"What is it, sweetheart?"

She sighed as he drew her close and held her gently but firmly. She sensed that he had known that this moment must come, had known that there were things that she would tell him when the time was right for her to do so, and that time was now. He remained quiet.

"Joel beat me." She felt the arms tighten and lips graze her hair. "I had no clue when we were dating. There weren't any former girlfriends to give any hint of what he was like. In fact, it later seemed odd that he had not really dated local girls that much considering what a good catch he seemed to be." She felt his body adjust closer to hers. "I thought that I was doing things that upset him, so I tried to be very careful about what I said, what I did, how I acted. But I began to realize that it wasn't me—he enjoyed it. There was really no true rage, just his made-up reasons to hit me—sometimes just once, but at other times it seemed as though he would never stop." She surmised his unspoken question and continued, "I was too ashamed to tell anyone. At first, I was ashamed to think that I must be doing something terribly wrong. Then I was ashamed for anyone to know that I had stayed with a man who abused me. Finally, I was ashamed for the scandal and gossip it would cause. So, I stayed. Of course, he always said how sorry he was and that it would never happen again. I am ashamed to think about how long I actually believed that."

He stroked her shoulder and kissed her cheek. "I promise that you are safe forever."

"I know that." She was quiet, gauging whether to end her story there. She sighed, then spoke barely above a whisper, "I knew he was going to kill me. Not that he hated me or especially wanted rid of me—he just wanted to do it. He had been so careful never to leave marks on me that would show. He was always the attentive, romantic husband in public, I knew he would find a way to do it and never be suspected. Then one morning I saw him watching me with a strange look in his eyes as I was coming down the stairs. Then I knew—today, or the next, or next week, or next month, I would suffer a fatal fall."

He buried his face in her hair where his tears were blotted. "The son-of-a-bitch is lucky he's dead!" Eudora had never heard him utter a curse word before.

"I knew at that moment that I had to get away to somewhere safe until I could figure out what to do, how to handle things. I had a passport because Daddy had taken me on one of his business trips to London. I don't think Joel even knew I had one. I waited until he was gone on one of his overnight trips, and I flew to France—to Provence. I stayed in a lovely old hotel in *St. Rèmy*. I spent days in the French countryside, painting."

She thought carefully about what to say next. "I met someone I could talk with. Someone who made me see that the fault was not mine. And that the guilt I had imposed upon myself was unwarranted. I was able to gain confidence and know how I wanted my life to be."

She knew he must have heard the touch of sadness in her voice. She was glad that he did not question. How could she have begun to explain what she had months ago come to realize had no explanation? This time, she had no desire or need to think further on the time she had spent in *St. Rèmy*. She did not think of a cottage or fields of flowers.

"I knew Joel would have given my family and everyone a plausible explanation for my absence. His ego would not allow anyone to suspect that I had left him. I came back, prepared to do whatever I needed to go do to get away from him. I had even made a list of the steps needed, but that was all ended when he hit that tree. I have never felt sorry, and I have never felt guilty about not feeling sorry. He got what he deserved, and I got my freedom with dignity. It was a relief, a release."

Cameron had never heard her speak so brutally. She surprised herself that she could speak so and was even more surprised that the words gave voice to deep-seated feelings finally acknowledged.

He held her tenderly through the night, making love once more as she woke and nuzzled against him.

Bright sunlight crept past the edges of the curtains as Eudora opened her eyes to find herself staring directly into his steel gray ones which crinkled at the corners as he smiled when he saw she was awake. She moved closer and nudged her face into his chest. He stroked her back with his fingertips. "You are so beautiful." He kissed her hair as she slid her body on top of his. "You realize that a maid is going to be here and knocking on our door any minute, don't you?"

"Oh, no, she won't. While you were snoring away, I had to get up once, so I hung out the Do Not Disturb sign!"

He looked at his wife then roared with laughter. "Looks like I have a lot to learn about you, woman. And I don't snore!"

"No, you don't, and we have all the time in the world to learn about each other."

Later as they lay side by side, fingers entwined, Eudora found the energy to speak. "I'm starving. I'm going to take a shower and you are not to come in with me or I shall faint from hunger before we get out of there!"

She ran for the shower, but finished quickly, not lingering. Cameron made an even quicker trip. When he came out, she had dressed in a simple sundress and sandals and tied her hair back with a ribbon. He pulled on slacks and a sport shirt, then they headed out to find sustenance.

They passed through lounges with marble floors and gold trimmed ceilings. One room contained an intricately hand-painted grand piano.

On one wall was a large painting of the hotel. Built in the fourteenth century, it had been the home of Andrea Gritti, the Doge. When being refurbished into a hotel, the elements and ageless charm had been retained.

Through floor to ceiling windows, they could see sunlight glistening on the Grand Canal which had looked so mysterious by moonlight. Also visible were many shops and the Rialto Market.

Breakfast time had long passed, being spent in activities other than eating. The Club del Doge restaurant was open for lunch. It was famous for cuisine that was wonderfully fresh, the ingredients being selected daily from the Rialto Market. The Masons sat enjoying their choices from the waiter's suggestions.

After eating, Cameron had another surprise for Eudora. He had hired a private car and driver for sightseeing. She danced with delight when she saw the car was a convertible. Cameron handed her another surprise, the beautiful silk scarf, that he had slipped away during the meal to purchase from the gift shop.

She tied the scarf over hair and slid to the middle of the back seat to sit with her husband's arm protectively around her.

The driver took the road along the Brenta Canal between Venice and Padua. They were able to view villas from the fifteenth to eighteenth centuries. Several of them had been designed by the architect Palladio. Eudora had always admired the symmetry of his designs.

They continued along the Brenta River to the village of Grassano del Grappa. They had time to admire some of the medieval architecture and visit a couple of small shops where Cameron bought her a little ceramic vase she admired. The local artists produced exquisite pieces.

They decided to have a light supper in the village before the drive back to their hotel. They savored the freshly made pasta and then were urged to sample the village specialty—grappa.

The stems, skin, pulp, and seeds left after squeezing the juice for wine-making were distilled to produce a brandy that is 35 to 60 percent alcohol.

There were different flavors, depending on the grapes that were used. All were tasty, all were potent!

The couple tried several samples, trying to be good sports. They purchased two bottles of their favorite to take with them and headed to their car in what they hoped was a decorous retreat. Their driver ushered them into the car where they sat with fingers interlaced and Eudora's head resting on her husband's shoulder.

The staff at the restaurant waved and bid them goodnight, calling after them what a wonderful couple they were, how in love, and that they must return in the future.

The remainder of the two weeks in Venice was filled with love and discovery of the beautiful country but more importantly, discovery of each other. It was a dedicated couple that headed home, declaring that they would someday return to Italy to see if the rest of it was as captivating as Venice.

They settled into a life that was filled with happiness and contentment. It was the rare moment, perhaps a breeze making a tree sigh, or the sweet scent of a flower, that would resurrect a fleeting memory of a time and place far away. The brief melancholy would pass, and her attention was returned to the present.

A baby! After four years of marriage, a baby. Martha Campbell Mason. Her daddy decreed that she is Maggie. I had to insist that she be given the formal version on her birth certificate. Cameron is a doting father and calls us his beautiful Southern belles—and treats us as such. Maggie is beautiful and growing so fast.

CHAPTER 24

"WELL, CAMERON, WE'RE BACK TO horses, are we?" Cameron just gave his wife a smile and what could in no way pass for a contrite look. He sensed, correctly, that her remark was in jest and that she was as pleased as he was with the little red Ford Mustang in the driveway. The gift was for Maggie's sixteenth birthday.

Eudora's comment referred to the gift for their daughter's tenth birthday six years previous. On that occasion, Cameron had shown up with a horse.

As with most young girls at one time or another, Maggie had been going through her love of horses stage. She had fallen in love with Marguerite Henry's books about horses. It was when she read *Justin Morgan Had a Horse,* that she became obsessed with the idea that she must own such an animal.

She had regaled them for weeks with the attributes of the Morgan breed. It was an all-purpose animal. It was a show horse, work horse, had a wonderful temperament and on and on until her parents begged her to find a new topic and her father had brought home a Morgan.

Maggie rode daily and cared for the horse without being reminded. She exhibited Justin at a local fair and brought home a blue ribbon. Her parents thought that might lead to her wanting to become involved in more showing events. Maggie, however, was content to hang the award on the door of Justin's stall and continue with their daily rides around the property.

"I promise this is the end of the horse theme." Cameron smiled at his wife, the winning smile that she could not resist. He bent to receive the kiss she was offering. He always marveled at how, after so many years of marriage, their kisses were still as thrilling and sparked as much desire as ever. "I love you so," he whispered as he held her close.

"I love you most." Her reply always touched his heart because he knew it came from hers.

"I had better get this car into the garage or there will be no surprise tomorrow." Maggie would be home soon and the look on her face would be priceless in the morning when she saw the Mustang in the driveway with a big red bow on top. The bow would be a cliché but would produce the same result as if it had been an original idea.

And the results were as predicted—squeals of delight—hugs all around—accepting the keys, then putting them on the personalized keychain, a special gift from her mother.

Maggie sat in the driver's seat and informed her parents that she wanted to take her driver's test the very next day. She had completed a driving course with a certified instructor who declared her ready to take the test and be set loose on the highways.

The proud parents stood with arms around each other and looked at their daughter, then at each other. Doctors had held out little hope that Eudora would conceive—a legacy from Joel. But they had beat the odds, Maggie was perfect and healthy, their miracle child.

CAMERON LEANED BACK IN HIS office chair. The call from his friend, the chief of police, had been the last straw, particularly since he knew his wife would be informed of its content by her friend, the chief's wife—she would know before he got home and he had better be prepared or face serious consequences himself. Eudora greeted him at the door as usual—nothing amiss, but he knew his wife—and he knew she had been filled in on all of the details of the call to him and the reason for it. The family dinner had passed as usual—Maggie chattering away about her day and Eudora and Cameron conversing in generalities. "Maggie, I would like to speak with you in my office." Cameron's tone held no clue as to what the conversation might concern, and Maggie had no reason to suspect anything amiss. She and her father often had conversations—perhaps to plan a surprise for her mother, discuss school, or any number of topics that could be the reason for this chat. Father ushered daughter into the room, entered and closed the door behind him. He indicated to her that she should sit on the couch that was situated in front of a wall of bookshelves. As he sat beside her, he noticed that her expression had changed slightly, showing a glimpse of concern.

He had been thinking of what he was going to say and knew that his handling of this issue was going to be critiqued by his wife—and he knew that she would indeed be within earshot, if not at the door they had just entered, then at the one that led out to the sunroom. Cameron glanced at both and wondered where the eavesdropper was waiting. He smiled because he had teased her about this trait being so out of character for her—not her usual lady-like behavior.

He turned a serious face to his daughter. "Maggie, I had a call from Chief Tallmadge today." He paused to give the statement time to have effect. He watched as Maggie's face fell.

"I'm sorry, Daddy, I just seem to have developed a lead foot." She raised her eyes.

Cameron did not let her off the hook. "You could have an accident and seriously injure yourself or someone else. It makes your mother and me worry each time you are out driving. It would concern parents of your friends who might be with you. It is irresponsible, Maggie, and so something has to be done."

"I know, and I truly am sorry, and I promise there will be no more speeding." She did look and sound contrite. "Are you going to take away my car keys?"

Cameron's heart almost melted—he loved this child and it was difficult for him to punish her. She had never been a difficult child, so discipline had been easy—but this called for action.

"I won't take your car because I believe you really are going to take this seriously and drive more carefully." He paused—he may not have been stern enough to satisfy the listener behind door number one or two. "However, Maggie, my dear, one more ticket and you can trade them in for a bicycle!"

As he stood, his daughter jumped up and hugged him. "No worries, Daddy." And she meant it. She turned a conspiratorial smile to him, "Do I need to tell Mama that you really read me the riot act and that I had to beg to keep the car?"

He laughed, "You know very well that your mother and I have no secrets from each other, and you also know that she has heard every word that transpired here."

They hugged each other again, laughed, and left the room with their arms around each other. Eudora was nowhere in evidence when they walked into the hallway.

"WELL, DID I PASS?"

"Whatever do you mean?" Eudora sat at her dressing table brushing her hair.

He could see the smile on the reflection of the woman in the mirror. He stood behind her and took the brush from her hand and began to stroke her hair.

She stood and turned to him, "With flying colors, as always. You were the perfect father, as you always have been. I'm sure the problem is solved. Our daughter is a responsible person, she just gets a little off course sometimes, but quickly gets back on track. We are truly blessed as parents."

"Yes, we are," he gathered her to him, "and Maggie is not my only blessing—you, my darling, are my first and continuing one." His kiss confirmed the validity of his statement. The kiss deepened as he swept her up into his arms and carried her to the bed.

I love my husband. I love my daughter. I love my perfect life.

CHAPTER 25

THERE WERE NO MORE SPEEDING TICKETS. There was a bigger drama brewing.

Eudora and Cameron were enjoying the tentative peace and tranquility that lulls all parents of teenagers. The world where all is sunshine and rainbows—beautiful music and harmony—then without any warning the cataclysmic end of that existence. The end of a teenage romance!

Maggie was an excellent and popular student. Her grades were straight A's. She played volleyball. She was a member of the glee club and drama society. Displaying an inquisitive mind and keen interest in many subjects had made her a favorite with her teachers. She had a group of friends who enjoyed the usual activities, shopping, doing each other's hair—and boys!

"Mama, Drayton St. Clair is a jackass!" And with that, the tranquility of the summer day was shattered.

"Margaret, watch your language." When she saw the outburst was to be followed by tears, Eudora moved quickly to take her daughter in her arms.

She led Maggie to a couch and sat beside her. Within seconds her daughter was sobbing against her. Her story was gulped out in short whimpers. The offending Drayton St. Clair, Maggie's first love, had told her that he thought they needed to break off their relationship before he headed off to college. Never mind that they had spent hours planning how he would go get established in college life then Maggie would join him after her graduation next year.

"Mama, I know it was those guys at the fraternities he has been visiting. They have convinced him that he will be expected to date sorority girls and not be obligated to a high school sweetheart!"

Eudora smoothed back her child's hair. "Well, he just doesn't know what he is giving up." Her heart ached for the girl. Her first heartbreak—a life's cruelty. For a few moments, Eudora was unable to push away the pain that came flooding back. That first lost love—it didn't matter if it was some callow high school boy disappointing a young girl or if it was fate, a twist of time, some unknown force tearing your heart from your chest. She swallowed hard and pushed the past back where it belonged.

"Mama, I am just going to die of embarrassment. Everyone is going to know he has dumped me. He is going to leave early for Old Miss, but he will be around for a few weeks and I'm sure to run in to him. I don't want to be laughed at or pitied! This summer vacation is going to be a disaster." The drama could only grow from here. The mother lioness needed to protect her cub.

Eudora settled Maggie into her room with sweet tea, then watched for Cameron to come home. He had barely set his brief case down before she presented him with their daughter's plight. He pulled his wife close, comforted and assured her that he could arrange an almost immediate solution—at least for the short term. They had been planning a summer trip anyway, so he had things in order at the bank to be able to be gone for a month.

Eudora contemplated her good fortune at having this man for a husband. Her heart was brimming with love as she joined him in going to give their unhappy child the news that within the week, they would be leaving to spend a month in a cottage on the beach near Biloxi.

"By the time we come back, sweetheart, the St. Clair boy will be on his way, and the only questions you will have to face will be about how much fun you had at the shore."

"Thank you, Daddy. Mama, I'm going to need some new bathing suits." Broken hearts can sometimes be temporarily soothed by simple distractions.

THE COTTAGE WAS LOVELY. THE interior was modern and there was a deck on the back with steps that led down to a short sea-grass lined path which emerged onto the sand. For the first week, the jilted teenager brooded, going for solitary walks on the beach or sitting on the deck staring at the water. As Eudora watched this, giving her daughter space, she could not help flashes of remembering her time on St. Simon's Island. She recognized the futility but also the healing power of walking by, or staring at, the sea.

Gradually, Maggie was joined on her walks by her father, and Eudora sat by her on the deck for short periods. Sitting quietly, Eudora would listen to the wind and the gulls and sometimes imagine that she could hear the tinkling of glass chimes.

"Mama, Daddy offered to break some of Dray's bones." She smiled, then chuckled, then was joined by her mother in a hearty laugh.

"Well, it may have been a symbolic offer, but it shows the depth of your father's love." She could imagine the conversation containing the offer, the father and daughter then sharing a laugh as mother and child were now.

NO LONGER A NEED FOR getting away from an uncomfortable situation, the trip became a true vacation. It was a time of renewal of relationships within the entire family. There were long talks between each parent with their child, and bonding family conversations. Eudora and Cameron shared special memories from their marriage and parenthood, but on a deeper level, they shared nights of passion and intimacy that renewed the love they experienced daily.

THE PARENTS WATCHED AS THEIR daughter made the acquaintance of some other teenagers at the beach. They smiled after one such encounter when they observed a tall, tanned young man walk a smiling Maggie up the beach then wave goodbye when they reached the short path that led to the cottage. She was still smiling as she joined them on the deck. Eudora went inside to get cold drinks for all of them, but she quickly ran back out when she heard Maggie scream, "Absolutely not!"

"What's going on?" She looked from the horrified face of her daughter to the puzzled one of her husband.

"I just suggested to Maggie that tomorrow we should all take a trip to explore Deer Island. It sounds like an interesting place, even said to be haunted." Cameron thought his planned excursion would make a good day trip.

"Haunted?" Eudora's look was skeptical.

"Haunted! I read a brochure about the place. A headless skeleton was found there once and a headless ghost of a decapitated pirate chases visitors!" Maggie was quite adamant in her protests and let her parents know that she did not appreciate their collective laughter at her outburst. "I don't care—I'm not going to Deer Island!" She flounced inside as the elder Masons tried to stifle their continuing chuckles.

"I suppose I owe her an apology, but you did laugh, too." Cameron looked toward his wife and their laughter broke out again.

Over dinner, both apologized for laughing and Maggie said that she had probably overreacted to both the haunting story and their reaction to her. Deer Island was not mentioned again. Instead, they decided that their trip would be to the Biloxi Light House. Eudora wondered if she would be drawn to this light as she had been drawn to the one on St. Simon's Island.

She smiled as she remembered the keeper's narration of the history of another light. This time it was Maggie who had done her homework and kept up a running stream of information about the Biloxi Light. While at first her mother kept relatively silent, her father asked numerous questions.

Eudora gradually relaxed as she responded to the history of the area. There was no need to climb to the top of the structure and look across the water hoping to find an answer that would not be there. She smiled as she realized it was not even the correct body of water. She joined in the conversation with her daughter and husband.

By the time Maggie had finished, the other two knew that the light had been built in 1848 and was unusual because it was built of cast iron. It had survived a hurricane in 1860 and another in 1868 and the light had continued to operate through both storms. The only time the light had been dark was during the Civil War, and that was to keep the Union navy from using it as a landmark.

Maggie finished her story by saying, "There was a legend started by magazine articles and spread by tourists that the tower of the light was painted black in 1865 to memorialize the assassination of President Abraham Lincoln. The unromantic reality was that it had been covered with tar to prevent it from rusting. It was painted white when it was built and is still painted white—no mourning period!"

"Well, thank you, madam guide. Do we owe you a fee for that informative tour?" Eudora was proud of her daughter's efforts in learning and sharing about the structure.

"Well, I wouldn't say no to a really good lunch."

"I can handle that," her father linked his arm through hers. "In fact, I noticed a small restaurant that looked as though it is frequented by a lot of the locals. I'm betting the food is good there." He was right. The three of them feasted on fresh gulf shrimp until all agreed that they should go back to the cottage for an afternoon nap and then take a long walk on the beach after their food had settled.

By the time the month was drawing to a close, tranquility had been restored to the Mason family, and if Maggie had any qualms about returning home, she did not voice them.

Upon the return to Booneville, they found that the offending Drayton St. John had indeed left to begin his college life. Maggie's friends and classmates were mostly concerned with finishing the summer with as much fun as possible before beginning their senior year and indeed were curious only about Maggie's adventures on her holiday. The parents congratulated themselves that the season had been salvaged from a morose beginning.

The couple had renewed their passion—their love only continued to deepen, but a dread began to niggle at the edge of Eudora's thoughts as she looked at the passing days on the calendar.

My drawing here of Alain is satisfactory but it is just charcoal on paper, as the original was only paint on canvas. I still see him as flesh and blood and warm to my touch.

CHAPTER 26

AUGUST 20,1975. EUDORA ARRANGED the day so that much of it could be spent alone. Maggie was away on a trip with a friend and her family. Cameron would be at the bank as usual, and she had given the staff the day off.

She thought about how the day might be passed, but in the end had not decided on anything in particular. The morning hours were filled with time spent in her favorite garden area—the place where wildflowers and lavender occupied most of the space. She allowed their colors and scents to draw her back to a time when they had filled her senses as she sat in a field in another time, another place. Bees and butterflies glided to their chosen blossoms. A bird was taking advantage of the water in the bird bath positioned in a far corner.

In the early afternoon she carried iced tea and sat in a chair under a huge magnolia tree. Attention was given to the cool sweet taste, to the moisture trickling down the side of the colorful aluminum tumbler, and even to the melting ice. The magnolia tree bore close inspection, large glossy green leaves, and the memory of perfect waxy white flowers. Eyes followed boxwood hedges marking their entire perimeter before moving to the arching canes of the roses within the enclosure.

Her mind hit an invisible barrier. There would be no more hiding by inventorying every inanimate object and plant within view. She had to face the significance of the day—the date that had stared at her from the calendar since early morning. The day that Alain Philidor had told her was his birthday.

She recalled the day she had painted his portrait. He had kept trying to distract her with a running conversation designed to make her smile and stop her work to playfully chastise him.

"Do you realize that you are dealing with a much older man here?" He gave her a grave look but could not keep his face somber.

"Well, you certainly don't kiss like an old man!"

"Oh, and you have kissed many old men?" They broke into laughter, and he had headed toward her.

"Oh no, you get right back there and let me finish. Just how old is this man I am in love with?" The admonition given, her voice became soft with the last question.

She saw the joy in his expression as he took in her declaration of love. His voice quivered as he said, "August 20, I will be thirty-one years old."

August 20. Why could there have not been a year mentioned? Just a simple number. The revelation could have changed everything. If they had both known about the horrible trick that time was playing on them, could they have found a way to resolve the situation so that they could have been together?

Don't do this. This had been resolved as much as possible on St. Simon's Island. This was laid to rest before this life she was living had begun.

She had spent glorious days with the man. The man she had loved—in another time. Today Alain would be born in her time—a newborn baby. Trying to think of him as an infant, then as a little boy, made her head hurt—it did not all fit together in any form that she could reconcile.

With a last look at her surroundings, she finished the rest of the tea and went inside to prepare supper and decided they should dine on the deeply shaded side porch. A rare cool spell would allow eating outside to be quite pleasant this evening.

Cameron arrived to find his wife in a long white sundress and a blossom in her hair. "What is the special occasion—a final night for just the two of us before Maggie returns?"

Eudora just smiled. "You have time to go up and change while I bring things out." Within minutes she heard her husband bounding back down the stairs.

"Eudora?"

"On the side porch. Well, don't you look handsome?" Her husband had changed into linen slacks and sport shirt.

"I had to try to look good enough to deserve you, though I've failed miserably—you look beautiful." He took her in his arms—their kiss was deep—full of love, born of times shared.

"If you will pour the wine, I'll plate up the salad—and guess what is under that cover." Her voice teased and her eyes danced.

"I don't have to guess. I can smell pork chops, and I know that wrapped in those napkins in that basket are homemade biscuits."

"I know we haven't had those things in a long time, I thought you were due for a small indulgence." He would not need to know that the pork chops were oven baked, but in a manner so that they tasted no differently than their fried relatives. Then she had scoured recipe books and magazines to find versions of the biscuits and pie crust that would be more heart healthy than the original versions. She smiled as her husband gave her a lingering kiss on the cheek and held a chair for her to sit.

They shared a leisurely dinner completed by a fresh peach pie. Cameron insisted that she relax while he carried the dishes into the kitchen. He came back and moved a chair to sit beside her. They were comfortable companions in the gathering dusk as fireflies began their evening light show.

"Thank you. Dinner was fantastic. I think I'll go in and do some reading. Are you ready to go inside?"

Eudora noticed that he had finished his wine, but she still had half a glass. "I think I'll just sit a little longer and finish my wine. Who knows when we'll get another evening this lovely?"

"That's true. Fortunately, the mosquitoes seem to have taken a vacation as well." He looked at his watch. "It's after nine, will you be up soon?"

"I won't be long. Don't wait up. You have been putting in such long hours lately, and I know you are tired." She took his hand and smiled up at him as he bent to kiss her before going inside.

CAMERON HAD FALLEN ASLEEP READING. Eudora gazed down at him as she carefully retrieved the book, placed it on his night table, and turned out the light. She made quick work of removing her makeup and brushing her teeth before she slipped between the sheets beside him.

Lying in the bed they had shared all these years, she could hear his quiet breathing and was once again glad that he had never had a snoring problem. The quiet, rhythmic sounds he emitted were an accompaniment to the beating of her heart.

The room was dimly lit by moonlight slanting through tall windows. The patterns made by the boughs of the willow tree outside were graceful, dripping arches with no wind blurring their mural on the wall.

Stretched full length, she lay on her back and stared at the ceiling. Hands lying at her sides, she had no desire to fidget with the sheet at her fingertips. Perfect stillness, perfect quiet—practically breathless, she waited. Sleep did not come, nor did she want it to. She knew that allowing for the difference in time zones, the moment she awaited had already occurred, but she wanted to live that moment here, where she was, where her life had been lived.

And then it began. The ancient clock in the hallway began to strike. *One—two—three—four—five—six.* She counted each strike in her mind— *seven—eight.* With each count her breathing became deeper, emotional— *nine—ten.* Her lips parted, and she longed to call out, but knew she must not. *Eleven.* She held her breath. *Twelve!* He lives! He is alive in my world. He exists. He is real. Sometime during this day, he has been born. He will have been handed from the doctor to a nurse who cleaned him, wrapped him in a soft warm blanket and brought him to the woman who bore him. She will have looked at him with love and awe, counted fingers and toes, then brought his rosebud lips to her breast.

Eudora slowly, quietly rolled onto her side, drew her knees up, touched fingertips to her lips as crystal drops coursed down her cheeks to stain her pillow. "You're alive." Her barely perceptible whisper was too quiet to reach the corners of the room where the void lurked.

CAMERON MASON LAY QUITE STILL and forced his breathing to continue with the deep soft resonance registered when he awoke earlier. He knew that Eudora was awake. There was tenseness in her body and a change at the last strike of the clock. Her whispered words were a puzzle.

Their life together had been filled with joy—happy and fulfilling. It wasn't that he had ever felt anything was missing, just that there was something that she had not shared. She had never told him in any detail about the time she was away, having fled from Joel. And he had never asked. He knew that she had left Booneville a fledgling with broken wings. There had been weeks after her return that were so dark that she had been driven to go away again, but she had risen from the ashes and returned a phoenix, rising to fly.

It had been only a casual mention of having met someone there who had helped in her resurrection—not whether it was a man or woman. He had occasionally wondered why she had not confided more to him about that time in her life but did not feel as though some sort of dark secret was being hidden. He felt an urge to pull her close but sensed that would cause consternation rather than giving comfort.

Both lay in stillness until sleep came.

The saying appears to be true. A son is a son till he takes a wife, but a daughter's a daughter all of her life. I believe Richard understands that but does not feel threatened by our closeness.

If I do not falter and try to imagine a young boy growing up in a distant land, life is kind.

CHAPTER 27

EUDORA HAD NOT TAKEN A stitch in the last ten minutes. Her thoughts were miles and years away from her sewing. They were all for her beautiful daughter, the little girl who had enchanted everyone, the teenager who excelled academically and in sports, the young woman who definitely had a mind of her own. The loving daughter who brought joy to their lives, was in love. She prepared for the moment when hurricane Maggie would be making a dramatic entrance.

She did not have long to wait.

Maggie came flying into the sitting room where her mother was pretending to sit quietly while also pretending to do needlework. "Mama, Daddy just scared Richard half to death. He told him that he was not giving his daughter away—not ever! I can imagine Richard's face. He must have turned ten shades of red before blanching white enough to faint!"

The women turned as the two men emerged from the study across the hall, both wearing broad grins. Before the younger one could faint as predicted, Camron Mason had clapped him on the back and welcomed him to the family. "I could never give my precious Maggie away, but I will be most proud to walk her down the aisle to become your wife."

Maggie ran into the hall where Richard covered his half of the space to take both of her hands in his and exclaim, "He gave his permission!"

Smiling, they walked to where Eudora stood. She stretched out her arms and the prospective bridegroom stepped forward to receive the embrace of his intended's mother.

Eudora patted his back, "Welcome to our family, Richard."

He turned back to Maggie. Holding hands, they walked out into the sunny garden.

"Cameron, you know that young man is very literal. Did you keep a straight face while torturing him? Maggie came in here quite frantic." Eudora looked up into the beaming face of her husband.

"Well, I couldn't resist—I knew Maggie had her ear glued to the door. I wonder where she got that trait?" Cameron smiled and Eudora feigned innocence. Her need to know had produced this, her most undesirable trait which seemed to have been passed on. "I only kept him on tenterhooks for a couple of minutes then gave him our full blessing—I knew I could speak for you, too."

"They are such a perfect couple. His calm, quiet spirit is a perfect counterpoint to Maggie's exuberance, he will take good care of her, and she will bring him lightness and joy. They will be very happy."

Cameron reached down, took the needlework from his wife's hands, and placed it on the side table. He pulled her to her feet and enfolded her in a tender embrace. "And you bring me lightness and joy and love and everything—more than I could ever have imagined. Eudora, you are even more beautiful now than the day we married."

They kissed lingeringly then walked to the window to look out at the young couple. Maggie was sitting on a garden bench while Richard knelt before her. Both had beaming faces. The parents turned away from the window so as not to intrude on this, the young couple's most personal and private moment.

Eudora remembered the day when Maggie had confided to her that Richard Harrison Walker III was *the one*. It was early in their relationship. Maggie was only twenty-one and Richard six years her senior. Any concerns the Masons might initially have had were quickly allayed. He was everything that any parent could hope for their daughter. He was established in his career, intelligent, kind, and loved Maggie with all his heart. They agreed that they couldn't have chosen better themselves.

The whirlwind began—*wedding plans!* While Eudora was quickly caught up with Maggie in plans, Imogene was the calm in the eye of the storm. Three Southern women and an event to plan!

The bride-to-be chose classmates from college for bridesmaids and Richard chose an equal number of friends as groomsmen. After that, his job was mainly to accompany Maggie to a cake tasting and then nod and smile appreciatively at the choices the ladies were making dealing with all of the details. He was allowed to make his tux choice—from two options.

The venue was not a choice. It would, of course, be the church where they all attended. The women were thankful for the beautiful sanctuary and immediately began drawing up plans with a florist for decorating the interior. A moonlight and magnolias theme had been unofficially chosen by the triumvirate. Garlands of magnolia leaves would be laid on railings. Here and there a glossy green leaf was to be sprayed silver. Roses, white and cream, would fill tall vases on pedestals, and be clustered with greenery on window ledges. Others would be tied in nosegays as pew markers. Countless numbers of silver and crystal candlesticks would be resting on every flat surface that was not for seating. They were of all shapes and sizes, including silver ones tall enough to stand on the floor. A small silver sconce topped the cluster of flowers at the end of each pew. Cream and white candles would give the sanctuary its evening glow as the time of the wedding had been set for dusk.

The day for choosing the wedding gown almost needed a printed program. The three met with Richard's mother for breakfast, then the four of them proceeded to the shop for an appointment to look at wedding gowns. Maya's Wedding Gowns was a permanent fixture in Booneville and its reputation had spread to the surrounding area. Maya had long since retired, but her daughter now ran the shop.

After the ladies were given comfortable seats and served tea, they were ready to see the procession of gowns. Several were brought for them to view and a few were chosen for trial. When Maggie mounted the small raised platform before them in the second gown, there was a deep intake of breath from all of the women. A simply cut gown of silk with lace accents—it was ideal. After examining all of the details and exclaiming over the perfection of the garment, a simple satin headband with a long wispy veil was chosen to complete the ensemble.

When Maggie emerged from the dressing room where final measurements had been taken so that the gown could be perfectly fitted, the three ladies on the sofa motioned for her to sit on a chair near them. Eudora pulled a flat velvet box from her bag.

"Maggie, your grandmother gave me these when I married. Now we want you to have them." The pearls had a luster that bore witness to having been lovingly worn by several generations of women.

"And my mother gave them to me when I married." Imogene's words brought tears to her granddaughter's eyes.

"And, Maggie, as Richard is an only child, you are the only daughter I will ever have. I am proud to give you this, which has been in my family for generations." This velvet box held a pearl and diamond broach which Maggie knew at once would be placed on the headband that anchored the veil.

The tears flowed freely from all of the women who dabbed at them with dainty handkerchiefs.

The following week the shop was invaded by Maggie and her bridesmaids. This time the drink was champagne. The girls tried and rejected several gowns, and joked that they hoped no one was filming their antics while having some frivolous fun with some of the designs. The final choice by consensus of the girls and approval of the bride, was a style that would complement the bridal gown. With an overlay of chiffon, the girls would appear ethereal floating down the aisle in their cream-colored gowns.

"DEARLY BELOVED...." THE MINISTER'S VOICE began the ceremony. Outside the chapel, dusk brought a time of magic. Inside the chapel the setting was a sea of white and cream, crystal and silver, and green magnolia leaves glistening in candlelight. The magic was the way the bride and groom looked at each other as they recited their vows. Love shone and was reflected in their eyes. Ladies made good use of lace handkerchiefs as the ceremony drew to a close. Eyes shed tears of joy and faces were wreathed in smiles of happiness.

Every detail was perfection. After the ceremony, while the guests were having cocktails in one room at the country club, the florist's staff had swiftly moved decorations from the church to fill the ballroom where dinner and dancing would take place.

Guests beamed as Mr. and Mrs. Richard Harrison Walker III danced the first dance. Then many guests' eyes misted as Cameron led Maggie to the floor for the father and daughter waltz. It was common knowledge that Maggie was a Daddy's girl, and the faces of the two of them played with so many emotions—love, giving, sharing, change, unchanging.

The society column of the local paper touted it as the wedding of the decade.

EUDORA AND CAMERON WERE HEARTBROKEN at her parents' news after the wedding. Both had cancer—different forms. The doctors were optimistic that both had been caught early and offered an encouraging prognosis for each, so the Campbells had held off with the news until after the wedding. Both had surgery—and the entire family felt the reports of the outcomes were promising.

Reminded that time could be fleeting, and every moment should be made to count, all members of the family took every opportunity to spend time together.

EUDORA AND CAMERON WANDERED THROUGH the house and wondered if this was what was meant by empty nest. They need not have concerned themselves. Maggie and Richard had taken up residence close by and were frequent visitors. While they had their own set of friends, those often overlapped with her parents' set as well. There was a wide circle that enjoyed each other's company and socialized frequently.

As had become their custom in the weeks following the wedding, the family was having Saturday morning brunch together when Maggie suddenly bolted from the table and ran for the powder room down the hall. Her parents looked concerned as Richard immediately got up to follow her. The Masons looked at each other and both began to smile.

"You don't suppose...?" Cameron began. "They've only been married three months."

"Well, my dear, not everyone takes as long as we did to start a family. I do believe that we are probably going to be grandparents."

"And we are going to be great-grand parents," Imogene beamed.

The young couple came back, Richard's arm around his wife. Maggie blushed and looked from one parent to the other, "Well, I see that we don't need to tell you our news."

Eudora rose to hug her daughter and Cameron pumped Richard's hand up and down. The Campbells had joyful hugs for the parents-to-be. They had one question, "When?"

"The doctor says I am about two months," Maggie sat back down, suddenly ravenous. As the others continued their meal, they wondered how a woman who could be so ill one moment could be so hungry the next.

"Mama, Grandmother, you might as well be prepared—you know how this place is. It may not be a small town in size, but you know there are lots of people who love keeping track of other people's business."

Eudora and Imogene did know. Eudora was quick with her reply, "Well, dear, don't let that worry you at all. Just enjoy your time while expecting this baby. Now, should we start planning a nursery?" The men laughed—if there was anything Southern women liked better than planning weddings, it was planning for a baby.

———————

THE LOCAL GOSSIPS HAD INDEED hurried to their calendars when it was announced that the recently married Walkers were definitely expecting an addition to their family. Some made clucking noises as they marked the date.

This would be the topic of gossip for quite some time. They were to be disappointed, some pleasantly and some sorely, when it happened that the Walkers had been married a full ten months when Eudora Imogene Walker was born.

Just as a doting father had decreed Maggie's name, a doting grandfather insisted that this child was Dory. Not only was it a diminutive of Eudora, but everyone could plainly see that this child was adorable. The third Southern belle had entered Cameron's realm of devotion. He would entertain the baby for hours and would crow with glee when she would reach for him as he entered the room. The women loved watching him with the baby and did not mind that they had probably been demoted to second and third places in his affection. Just wait until she was old enough to start showing a bit of willfulness, of which the women were pretty sure they could already see a few telltale signs—a change of facial expression, a tilt of the head—oh yes, Grandpapa was in for some surprises.

The family circle was enlarged. Richard's parents came to visit often. Life was full—and good.

———————————

EVEN THE BLESSING OF A new baby could not soften the blows which soon followed. Both of Eudora's parents lost their battles with cancer. The disease had reappeared in both and their decline had been rapid. No amount of medicine, prayer, or care slowed the progress. They were gone. The shock left her reeling. After the last funeral, she took to her room, inconsolable.

Cameron brought her trays to tempt her to eat—most times, she could not. Her constant thoughts involved loss. She had been so close to her parents, and to lose them both in such a short period of time and so quickly had crushed her spirit. She cried until there were no more tears. Worst of all, other thoughts of loss came crowding back. Or at least they tried to.

She knew that she would be lost—would lose the life she had built—if she allowed herself even to begin to imagine a young boy growing up in a distant land.

She reminded herself that she had a husband she loved, a family who needed her, and a granddaughter she had not seen in a week. She knew Maggie and Richard were downstairs with the baby. She got up, pulled on slacks and a sweater, brushed her hair, added a touch of blush and lipstick, then headed down the stairs. Her parents would be smiling in approval as she made this trek.

Life goes on. The thought struck her that she had made that a truth to live by over the years. She smiled as she reached the bottom of the stairs and walked toward her family.

———————————

Eudora felt blessed. Maggie and the baby visited almost daily. She saw Dory's first smile, the one that was *definitely* not gas. She watched with pride as her daughter cared for the baby. A shadow would cross her face only at times when she would think, *If only Mother could see this.*

Life seemed to have turned another corner—Dory was the only baby that filled her thoughts. No visions of a little boy far away intruded, and the man he would become ceased to haunt her.

Holding Dory, entertaining her, was a joy surpassed only by the pleasure of watching others with her. While Maggie was the perfect mother, Richard and Cameron outdid themselves in father and grandfather roles. Both spoiled the child shamelessly. If the baby showed the slightest sign of distress or boredom, both would rush to pick her up or offer some sort of distracting entertainment. Eudora would jokingly admonish them, and Maggie finally had to declare a mortarium on gift giving. The nursery was crowded with every sort of toy a child would ever want or need from birth to long past childhood.

Days of perfection, lives fully blessed continued for the extended family.

———————————

STATE TROOPERS WERE AT THE door and again ushered inside. Sounds—were there sounds—or was there a vacuum of silence? Were they saying something? Why was she standing in an empty space—where was the furniture? The room spun slowly, Cameron's arms were around her and lowering her to the sofa. That is all that she remembered from those first awful minutes.

A cool cloth—Cameron's strong encircling arm restored a semblance of reality. Why were there tears running down his face?

"No! No!" And then she was screaming.

Maggie and Richard Walker had been killed instantly when a drunk driver crossed the center line and hit their car head-on. The officers spoke more, but that was the only statement she remembered.

People would speak of the tragedy and marvel at the miracle within the horror. Securely fastened into her carrier in the back seat, their baby did not suffer even a scratch.

The Masons mourned the loss of their daughter but immediately set about caring for their orphaned granddaughter. Richard's parents were older and agreed that the Masons should be the ones to raise the baby.

In reality, they were parents again.

CAMERON WAS THE ROCK NECESSARY to Eudora's survival. But Eudora was a Southern woman. She quickly gathered her strength and set about taking care of the baby. They parented together, she and Cameron. Their marriage had grown stronger through the years and now steel girders were added to the structure as they supported each other.

Cameron was able to tailor some of his hours at the bank to fit the family schedule. Eudora was the daytime caregiver, but Cameron was there in the evening to feed Dory dinner and together they made bath-time an event.

Dory was a beautiful baby, sweet and displaying a vivacious personality. In looking at some of Eudora's old family photographs, Cameron noted that Dory grew daily to look more and more like her grandmother at each stage in her life. Eudora demurely denied the idea but secretly acknowledged to herself that it did seem to be true.

That realization brought delight that she kept to herself. It also brought a dread that nibbled at the corners of her happy world. Flashes of the troubling times in her own life would bring a streak of gray to her sunny day.

Dory was being raised in an environment much as her own had been. Though it was grandparents, rather than parents who were her immediate family, the dynamic was the same. Her parents were only the beautiful young couple in the photograph on her dresser and in the grand painting hanging by the staircase.

Invariably, Eudora worried that perhaps something in the way she was being brought up might make her vulnerable to men of Joel's character. Logic told her there was no connection, but logic can be lost when concerned about loved ones.

Could some weird time circumstance happen to her as had happened to Eudora? There was no end to imagined unpleasant possibilities.

One day as she sat watching Dory chasing a butterfly in the garden, she realized that she was letting doubt and worry rob her of some of the joy of watching this child grow. She borrowed no more trouble, but treasured every minute of the life she was given.

"CAMERON WAS THE ONE WHO cried." Eudora was having lunch with her friend, Sarah Parker. The women were years apart in age but the children they nurtured had brought them together. They had discovered that they had similar interests and had become good friends.

"I knew today would be an emotional experience, but I had no idea that Cameron would take it so hard. I didn't think he was going to let go of her hand so that she could actually go into that kindergarten room!" Eudora smiled.

Actually, Cameron's reaction had made today easier for her to keep her composure—couldn't have Dory totally embarrassed on her first day of school.

"Finally, Dory said, 'Dad, you have to let go of my hand, my teacher is waiting!' Cameron just looked at me and we both broke out laughing. He let her go but cried as we walked to the car. I never loved that man more than I did at that moment."

Sarah's eyes misted. "He is one in a million. You are a blessed woman. Tell me though, has it ever bothered you that Dory calls you Gran but calls Cameron, Dad?" She had never heard the explanation that Eudora began to relate.

Eudora laughed. "Well, she actually began calling him Granddad, but she said that she could only get the Gran part out and then I would quickly jump in to answer! She decided that if he were ever to get to speak for himself or at least answer first, she would have to change the way she addressed him—he became Dad, with the Grand part to be understood."

It was Sarah's turn to laugh. "I can't believe you have never told me that story. I'm sorry I missed you at the school. I had my own separation anxiety moment this morning."

Sarah was a single mother and Eudora thought again of how fortunate she was to have Cameron with her.

The two finished their lunch then set out to begin their days in their empty houses. Neither felt sad as there was the promise of little girls who would come home full of excitement and stories about their first day at school.

The years have flown by. Years of conferences, games, concerts, all filled with Dory. Sweet disposition, straight A student, athletic ability, beautiful soprano voice—and oh yes, unabashedly bragging here—full scholarship to Old Miss and being rushed by Kappa Kappa Gamma!

CHAPTER 28

JULY 4, 2000. THE TURN of the century. Cameron Mason was reflecting on the celebrations that had been staged around the country for the new year, and now the Independence Day celebrations were no less spectacular. The Masons had hosted a huge party. Close friends, acquaintances, and business connections swelled the ranks of attendees. Dory's friends spent the afternoon around the pool, alternately sunbathing then playing games after someone had been tossed into the water to start another round of raucous fun. Young and young at heart danced under the stars, and when the night sky deepened, a fireworks display lit up the heavens.

"The party was spectacular, Eudora. You absolutely outdid yourself with this one." After the last guests were gone, they settled into chairs by the pool. Cameron had turned off the lights in the area so that there was a clear view of the myriad of stars above them.

"It was the catering company and our staff who should really be congratulated." Eudora had always been quick to allocate credit where she knew it belonged.

"I know, but you're the one who planned every detail and saw to its execution."

She laughed, "Execution. That sounds so sinister!"

He joined her laughter, "You know what I mean. The plans were fabulous, and you are the most perfect hostess I know. How you can combine so many different groups of people and have them all enjoy the party and each other is amazing."

"We do it together, my darling. Cameron, looking back on our life together, what we've gone through, what we've overcome, what we've accomplished—sometimes it almost seems like watching from a distance—seeing some other people."

He rose, took her hand, and pulled her up to him. Their kiss was long and deep. Smiling and looking deeply into her eyes he said, "I'm glad this is not some other people—I'm glad this is us."

"Agreed! You know, I think I'm ready for bed now—tired has finally caught up to me."

"I'll be up soon. I'm just going to be sure everything is closed up properly."

Within fifteen minutes, he climbed the stairs to find his wife already in bed and asleep. He brushed his teeth and then climbed in beside her.

Unable to fall asleep, Cameron looked toward his sleeping wife and smiled. A wisp of hair that had fallen across her face was tenderly brushed aside. Soon there would be another milestone—in only a few more years, they would celebrate their golden wedding anniversary. Fifty years and each of them filled with more blessings and joy than any man could have wished for.

It was to be the last thought and feeling, of which he was aware. The steel bands that encircled his chest tightened with such speed that he was unconscious almost immediately and stopped breathing entirely within two minutes. He had tried to call out, but any sound was only imagined. *He slipped away quietly in his sleep* was how the article in the newspaper would read.

EUDORA WALKED THROUGH THE DAYS in a numbed state preparing for the funeral. She functioned by rote. How different this service was to be from the one for her first husband. That one had brought a welcomed end. This one left her heartbroken and alone again.

Unbidden, Alain Philidor once again entered her thoughts—he could claim time there now as it would not be an infringement on a living husband. Her two losses—Alain and Cameron—somehow equals.

One had been her passion, the other her lifetime love. Now both were gone, both had left her. Not true, she could not blame Alain. He had not left her. Indeed, it was she who had caused him pain. She knew he had suffered, had not understood. How could he? He did not know she was not of his time. Memories, blurred at the edges by distance, sometimes caused her to wonder if it had all been a dream or perhaps a fantasy her tortured mind and body had conjured in order to survive the ordeal of her first marriage.

She could not blame Cameron. He had been so loving, so patient. He had been her companion and lover. They had shared a child and raised a grandchild together. She had never cheated him of her love and devotion, but there was a part of her that had not been there to give—it had been left in another time, another place.

She could not blame them. Neither would have chosen to leave her. She could only celebrate their lives and be grateful that they had shared them with her.

THE WIDOW LOOKED TO WHERE the cemetery workers sat under a distant tree. They had been quietly and patiently awaiting her departure. She had sent everyone away, including Dory. She needed this time alone, but it was time to go now. She took a deep breath, stood, and gently dropped the rose downward onto the casket. Slowly she stooped, gathered a handful of dirt, and let it drift downward onto the wood below, "Dust to dust...." She held her head high, then turned and walked toward the car where a driver opened the door for her, and Dory reached out to enfold her grandmother into a gentle embrace.

BOONEVILLE, MISSISSIPPI, IS AN ENCHANTED place to be in

autumn. By October, leaves of the maples are vibrant, rivaling the sweet gums. Brilliant green of stately pines provides relief that sets off the colors of their deciduous neighbors. Gentle breezes swirl the fallen gems around ankles and nostalgia runs rampant. Eudora sat on a bench in the garden, deliberately giving freedom to thoughts and feelings that had been banished for so many years.

How long since I left Alain and returned? There is no way to calculate. Do I use my time, his time, or was time even involved? Was it only a moment that existed between one breath and the next? Did we love in the blink of an eye that should have been an eternity?

Autumn had settled a reflective, melancholy cloak about her shoulders. She could not always find words to explain the feelings she was experiencing. Was it a wish for something that no longer existed, maybe never did? Was Alain only a dream? She refused to believe that. She had thought that once their times overlapped, she would feel something more—a connection, but she didn't. She remembered only the man and could never visualize the child. Somehow even trying to think of him as a youngster, playing, growing, eluded her.

Her thoughts led her over and over again to his name, *Alain*.

I should know better than to let my thoughts start down this path, but I can no more resist the journey than I could resist the man. I have relived a thousand times, every moment we spent together. There are not enough smiles in the world to erase his, not enough warm and tender embraces to make me forget the passion we shared. Not enough love to free me from the things he made me feel, and no incentive to want to forget. I could manage a reasonable perspective while Cameron lived, but with him gone, there is nothing to rein in my memories and unbridled, they run as free as the horses we once watched on the Camargue.

Alain was my dream—our love was my dream—our future was my dream. That fateful night when I faced the horrible reality that we were of different times, I knew I had to stay with him. In the garden, I removed my wedding ring and threw it away—I turned to go back inside, but something happened, and our lives were forever ripped apart.

The leaves are garnets, rubies, amethysts, topazes, and emeralds as they lie on the ground and are joined by the diamonds falling from my eyes. Autumn is a sadness, a beautiful pain. As long as I can feel that I am alive, and what we shared is alive. We had moments, but not years, and memories are all that extend that time. Alain is now a young man—but I am an old woman....

...to everything there is a season....

CHAPTER 29

"WELL, MISS EUDORA IMOGENE WALKER, you have laid out a proposal so well prepared that you think it will be impossible for me to reject it." Eudora, the elder, looked at her granddaughter with mock sternness. Dory had presented a plan for the two of them to, as she put it, road trip together.

"Gran, you have traveled up and down the east coast, even gone to Europe a couple of times, but have never seen any part of the beautiful country west of the Mississippi River." The opening volley was fired—a large part of the country never visited.

Eudora looked at her granddaughter, as she was often told, a miniature of herself. She smiled. It was rather satisfying to see a reflection of herself passed on to a new generation. Maggie had looked so much like her father that Eudora seemed completely left out—and that was okay with her. But now here was the child she had raised, more like another daughter than a grandchild, who was her likeness in temperament and personality as well as appearance.

Dory continued her pitch, "We'll start with Bryce Canyon and Zion National Parks, then drive south to the Grand Canyon, Painted Desert, Petrified Forest, and then finish our trip in Las Vegas."

Eudora could not resist the urge to tease, "Ummm, I didn't realize that Las Vegas has been designated as a national park." Her eyes twinkled and she could not hold back laughter.

"Gran, you are an evil woman."

Eudora was familiar enough with the current vernacular to know that she had just been paid a high compliment. "Dory, this may surprise you, but I think this is a wonderful idea, and I will be happy to let you do all of the planning."

"Well, that is mostly done. All you have to do is pack. You should take comfortable clothing and walking shoes for the daytime. We won't be doing enough walking to tire you out, but we will do what you feel like. Then for evenings, things for casual dining, except when we get to Las Vegas. For that, pack some fancy duds. We will paint the town, so to speak."

Dory's enthusiasm was contagious. "When do we leave?" She was already onboard with the idea.

"Next Tuesday. I'm off now to do some last-minute shopping. Is there anything you need?" Dory was obviously relieved that she had received no resistance to her idea.

"There is nothing at all that I can think of." She watched as her grand-daughter left with a bounce in her step. She knew that the girl had been par-ticularly concerned about her of late, and Eudora had to admit that she had not been her usual energetic self. More and more since Cameron's death, she had not found excitement in the usual activities that filled her days.

Her *days*. Not her life. Her life... exactly what was that now? A path of thought she would not travel. Dory was in her life and that was enough. Not just enough, happy and fulfilling. This was the most important lesson that life had taught her. Happiness was living in the real time of what is. So many times, circumstances had snatched away the people who brought happiness to her life. Each time she had teetered on the brink of total despair and had only survived due to her strong will and trust in a power higher than herself. Herself. Life had taught her that she was enough. The people in her life had been gifts to love and to love her back, but not re-sponsible for her happiness.

Chiding herself that she was getting dangerously close to a wallow, she walked to her desk and began preparing a list. She had become quite fond, even dependent upon making lists. This one was comprised of the three cat-egories of clothing Dory had mentioned, plus the extras she would need, nightgowns and other things—on a whim she added a swimsuit—surely some of their accommodations would have a pool.

DORY CONGRATULATED HERSELF AS SHE placed the fresh flowers on her grandfather's grave. "Well, I did it, Grandad. She didn't even offer any resistance to going on the trip. I might have worried because she didn't quite seem like her old self, but this was not a loss of spirit, more like a sereneness that is comforting. She is okay. She misses you, but she is okay." Saying it aloud was a reassurance. She had been concerned about her grandmother—at times wondering if she had lost the will to live. She no longer worried. This was the Gran she knew, the Gran who had raised her.

With a farewell to her grandfather, she set off to do the afore-mentioned shopping. Enjoyable hours were spent replenishing her wardrobe and picking up a few surprises for her grandmother.

She returned home, finished her packing and had dinner with Eudora, then sat with her in the sun room to have wine.

She watched as Eudora sipped the white Grenache and wondered at the slight smile that crossed her face. "Does that wine remind you of your trip to France all those years ago?"

Eudora jumped at her words, then smiled again, "Actually, it does. Taste is a sense that can recall memories. I can see the beautiful flowers, the walls of the ancient city, and smell the freshness of the countryside."

Dory sensed there might be something more, but her grandmother was finished with her commentary on the topic. Eudora had raised her from a baby and had shared everything with her—well, almost everything. From her teenage years, the girl had often felt that Gran held something for herself, not anything that would be of concern to her family, but something. There had been little clues, and Dory had concluded that it had something to do with her trip to France. Maybe Gran had an adventure there that she didn't want to share with anyone. Well, that was all right. Everyone should have things that were only for themselves.

Dory had her own for herself thing. It had to do with the handsome new young teller at the bank. She knew at a young age that she wanted to follow Cameron into the banking business. She had studied finance in college and started working at the bank. Her skill and ability to deal with people had earned her promotions. Her position as a supervisor had become a small barrier when Andrew Smith-Palmer had been employed as the newest teller and she was his supervisor.

She had inherited her grandmother's uncanny ability to know when a man was interested though nothing was outwardly apparent. She knew that Drew was definitely interested even though he had given no outward indication of that interest. When she returned from this trip, the situation would need to be addressed to see what might be possible. Andrew Smith-Palmer—Dory smiled. "I believe this is the first person I have known with a hyphenated last name."

EUDORA WAS THOUGHTFUL. SHE HAD caught Dory's look during the wine discussion. There had been thoughts of having a conversation with her granddaughter but the idea was discarded. It was too much to go into. And it would never be just one conversation—it would be there just lying in wait to be brought up again and again until all of the old hurt, disbelief and uncertainty would come flooding back and erase the acceptance and peace that had been purchased at an exorbitant price. Better to leave that for after....

This trip. Dory was so excited, and her excitement had definitely sparked Eudora's interest. She found herself looking forward to the travel. They would be flying to Salt Lake City, thus avoiding extra days of driving. That was good because long days in a car were not easy for her. She remembered when that had not been the case. She had driven two days straight to get to and from St. Simon's Island. That seemed distant now, but if she closed her eyes, she could remember sitting on that porch watching the sea and listening to the enchanting tinkle of the glass wind chime. She had found salvation there. Not only had she grown spiritually, but also, or perhaps because of that, she had grown in confidence that a wonderful and fulfilling life lay ahead of her. And it had. But she could not help but wonder what was next. She must be careful not to encroach on Dory's right to a life of her own. She must attune herself to what was a closeness with her granddaughter as opposed to what would be taking away time that Dory should be using to pursue her own destiny and happiness.

"Enough deep and serious thinking!" She laughed at herself and prepared for bed.

—————————

A FRIEND OF DORY'S DROVE them to the airport and saw them safely inside the terminal. Since as much as possible had been taken care of ahead of time, check-in was uneventful. They were in the air and the captain had just turned off the seatbelt sign when Dory decided it was time to inform her companion about the little quirk having to do with the next part of their journey. Eudora was mildly interested but exhibited no concern about the information she received. Her surprise was a little more than mild, however, when she actually saw the plane for the next leg of their journey after Salt Lake.

The small plane was parked on the tarmac with stairs pushed up to it for boarding. Both passengers managed quite easily and simply chalked it up to a new experience. Eudora did consider it an opportunity to tease her granddaughter.

"Well, at least we didn't have to climb up a ladder." With a sideways glance she noticed that Dory looked a little worried, so Eudora quickly assured her that there had been no problem at all. "I take it that the Cedar City airport is rather small."

"Yes, actually it was built originally as a military training air strip with a dirt runway. Of course, it is paved now and there is regular commuter service in and out."

Both women were glad that the short flight was uneventful. The landing was smooth, again stairs were rolled up to the plane and then inside the terminal luggage was collected. Dory left Eudora on a bench in the crisp high desert air. It was only a matter of minutes before she pulled up in the rental car, loaded their bags into the trunk, collected her grandmother, and drove to their hotel for the night.

————————————

THE VIEWS WERE AWE-INSPIRING as they approached the entrance to Bryce Canyon National Park. After a stop at a small visitor center, they left armed with maps, brochures, and a bag of snacks and bottles of water. The park offered miles of hiking trails, but none were the level of physical activity desired by the two women. They opted for the scenic drive that stretched over thirty miles.

With Dory doing the driving, Eudora became the tour guide. She shared the information that the fantastic formations were the result of water freezing and expanding in cracks in the rocks, forcing the limestone to split apart. What geologists designate as slot canyons, fins and spires called *hoodoos,* appear as magical structures to amazed tourists.

The car was often pulled off the road at spots designated as a scenic view. Eudora and her granddaughter would point out particular formations, but most often they stood or sat in silence, overcome by the power and beauty of the landscape.

One of nature's formations reminded Eudora of the manmade structure she had visited in France. As she gazed into the distance, Alain sat beside her. A gentle breeze was his breath on her neck. She closed her eyes and allowed herself to see his face. It was a moment of solace, no residual pain.

"Dory, I cannot thank you enough for this trip." She stepped to hug her granddaughter who grasped her close and held her in a tight embrace.

"I love you, Gran." The younger woman's eyes were bright with tears that threatened to spill. "I don't think we are very far from Rainbow Point which is the highest in the park. That should be a good place to have the snacks that we picked up at the visitor center."

That prediction proved to be true. They ate in silence, looking at the panorama before them.

Dory broke the silence, "Ebenezer Bryce was right. It's one hell of a place to lose a cow." She spoke of the rancher who had purportedly given that answer when someone had asked him what he thought about all of those big canyons that backed his ranch. Evidently his cattle had a propensity to wander into the area, making it difficult to find them. The people of the valley called the place Bryce's canyon and the name stuck.

It had been a long day, so their course was set for tonight's accommodations, the Bryce Canyon Lodge. Situated on a mesa close to the rim of the canyon, it has housed travelers since 1924. The original two-story stone building contains an arts-and-crafts designed lobby with its large rubble masonry fireplace. The women noted that sitting in front of it later while having a drink would be a fine idea. The building also housed the dining room, gift shop and other services offered to guests.

The guest cabins were built a few years later. They sit in a pine grove and while things such as bathrooms have been updated periodically, the stone fireplaces, wood paneling, and the exteriors have been little changed. Dory and her grandmother unpacked the things they needed for the night then walked along a paved pathway to the main lodge to have dinner.

Back at their room, Eudora changed into her nightgown, then put on a warm robe and went out onto the porch of the cabin. She pulled a chair close, leaned on the peeled log railing, and gazed into the moonlit landscape. She looked up as Dory joined her. "Your grandfather would have loved this place."

"Why did you never travel to this part of the country?"

"We never really thought about it. Our trips and vacations were never that far from home. Well, except for our honeymoon in Venice, and then that next Christmas we spent in New York. After that, we just seemed to have everything we needed close by. Except the seashore, of course, and even the Gulf coast isn't that far away." Pictures flashed in her mind, Maggie, then Dory playing in the sand—Cameron building sandcastles with them wonderful times—loving times. They decided to linger at the location for another day. They went for one short drive but mostly relaxed and enjoyed the beauty of the area and hotel. Several of the hours were spent in just sitting quietly on the porch.

THE WOMEN WERE DRIVING THE last few miles out of the park when Eudora broke into uncontrollable laughter. Dory braked suddenly and looked at her grandmother who managed to reassure her immediately that there was nothing wrong. "It just suddenly hit me what an odd name *hoodoo* is for those beautiful spires. I wonder how geologists came up with that name. is it a Native American term, or what?"

"Well, you can do a search for that information later. You scared me half to death!"

"I'm sorry, I'll share the thought before my reaction the next time."

"It is pretty funny, actually." She smiled at the term as well as her grandmother's reaction to it.

During the next three hours they made one stop to use the facilities and walk around to stretch their legs. When they reached Zion National Park, again their first stop was at a visitor center for the maps and brochures. Once more they opted for the scenic drive rather than hiking. Frequent stops to look at the view from particular vantage points provided enough exercise for the day. Eudora watched the surroundings carefully when exiting the car as some of the information had informed her that the park held twenty-nine species of reptiles.

"I'm sure that includes a lot of harmless little lizards and things like that."

"And I'm certain that I don't want to encounter any of them, harmless or not. I'm pretty sure this is also rattlesnake country!" She gave an exaggerated shudder. Even though they had their importance in the ecosystems, she had never been able to develop an appreciation for snakes. She couldn't even stand to look at pictures of them!

The drive revealed more of nature's wonders. Colors changed from cream to pink to red on the massive sandstone cliffs. Much of the scenery was a reminder of what they had seen yesterday, yet there were differences, minute or massive.

"It's like nature set out to do wonderful painting and carving in this whole section of the country." Dory's words voiced what was in her grandmother's mind.

"It is marvelous, isn't it? I don't know how people could see marvels like this and not believe in God." Eudora spoke quietly, reverently.

By late afternoon, the travelers were ready to seek their accommodations for the night. At the Zion Lodge, hotel rooms were available, but Dory had once again booked one of the cabins. This lodge had been built during the same time period as the one at Bryce Canyon and had also retained its rustic charm.

When they returned to their cabin after having dinner at the Lodge, they found a fire burning brightly in their fireplace. "Did you arrange for this?" Eudora queried her granddaughter.

"Guilty. I knew it would be nice to break the evening chill at this elevation."

They donned sweaters and sat on their porch enjoying the crisp air of the high mesa, then went back inside to the warmth of their room and beds.

Eudora beamed, thanked the gift giver, then donned the soft flannel nightgown, one of the surprises Dory had bought for her.

AFTER A LEISURELY BREAKFAST AT the Lodge, the women visited the gift shop, and each found handcrafted items to purchase.

"Gran, we have a longer drive today, but we will stop often to get out of the car and move around if you need to stop, just let me know." Her tone showed her concern for the older woman.

"I'm sure wherever you stop will be fine." Eudora appreciated the consideration. She was thankful for the fact that they now shared a close relationship as adult women as well as the close family bond that had grown continually throughout their lives.

The seven-hour drive did not seem that long. The ever-changing scenery was punctuated by the stops for rest and food. Conversation during the time in the car was minimal as the scenic wonders commanded their attention.

When they entered Grand Canyon National Park, they drove directly to their lodging. El Tovar was another historical hotel from the early nineteen-hundreds. Tired from their drive, the women ate an early dinner then retired for the night.

THEY SLEPT LATE THE NEXT morning then opted for a late breakfast.

"Darling, if you don't mind, could we wait a while to start sightseeing? I was reading one of the brochures and found that right next door is the Hopi House. It's an authentic Pueblo style building with a huge gift shop and a Native American art gallery."

"I think that's a wonderful idea." Dory was always open to shopping and the shops of the area were a treasure trove of unique handmade items.

The art gallery was a moving experience. Both women were engrossed in the depictions of the Native American cultures. Talented artists skillfully portrayed the daily life, spirituality, and beauty of the peoples who had resided in the area for hundreds of years.

When they finally entered the gift shop, the array of native arts and crafts available for purchase tempted both beyond resistance. They bought silver jewelry and pottery. "Now what are you going to do with that?" The Kachina doll Eudora was examining drew a skeptical look.

"I'm not buying it! They look rather frightening but are somehow quite beautiful. I find them mystical. What I am going to buy is that Navajo rug that I have looked at and passed by at least three times. I think it will be quite wonderful in the upstairs hallway."

"I'll speak with the customer service department to have the rug and our pottery shipped home. Don't buy anything else big while I am doing that." Her mock sternness drew a smile.

The gallery and shopping had filled the morning and until just after noon. They decided on lunch and then a rest in their room.

After an hour of napping, Eudora pronounced herself ready for seeing the Canyon. They drove the route along the south rim. Late in the afternoon they stopped and sat on a low stone bench to watch the changing landscape as the sun dipped lower.

As the view changed from minute to minute, Eudora thought about how life was much the same. The years with Cameron had seemed to fly by so quickly—there had been many of them but now they seemed condensed somehow. Experience had taught her not to fall apart after losing him, but she also knew that she would never cease to miss him. There would never be anyone else. She had been blessed with two great loves in her life. When put into perspective, the relationship with Alain had not been allowed to progress, so it had been infinitely more difficult to accept that loss. It had nearly destroyed her. The loss of Cameron was a natural progression of life. It did not mean that she missed him any less. There had been so much more time with him—a life—a wonderfully full life.

THEIR NEXT DAY WAS SPENT exploring more areas of the Canyon and another night at the hotel there. They extended this to yet one more night so as to have more time in the art gallery. They did, however, agree to resist going to the gift shop again.

The following morning, they drove southeast to reach the areas known as the painted desert and the petrified forest. As this had required the greater part of the day to drive, they spent the night at a hotel close to the entrance of the Painted Desert National Park. The following day was spent driving through that park and then the Petrified Forest National Park.

The colors, the formations, again while having great or subtle differences, were tied together with the feeling that there must have been a master sculptor and artist at work.

"That petrified wood is fascinating." They had read about its formation in complete awe. "Over two hundred million years old—and these were living organisms—it's like looking right into the very distant past. It is sad that so many pieces were carted away before the designation protecting them."

"So now, they are literally like giant crystals. The range of colors is amazing." Eudora paused, "I just realized it is the colors that speak to me. The formations are grand beyond belief, but it the colors, the tints, the shades, the idea that perhaps there are even colors we don't see because we have no name for them, no way to recognize them by calling them by name. I'm not making sense, am I?"

"I understand exactly what you mean, Gran. I hadn't thought in those terms, but I know just what you mean." The women were quiet, both lost in thought and reflection until they reached their hotel in Flagstaff, Arizona, for the night.

EUDORA AWOKE EARLY THE NEXT morning. She looked at her granddaughter still sleeping in the next bed. Her eyes glistened and her heart was filled with love and pride. Fate had taken so many things from her but had left a living reminder of so much that had filled her life. Dory was Maggie's daughter, Cameron's granddaughter, her lasting connection to the two of them.

Dory opened her eyes and saw her grandmother looking at her. "Well, you're awake early. Did you have trouble sleeping?"

"No, I slept quite well, but I have been thinking about something and I hope you won't be disappointed. I want to go home. We have seen so many natural wonders. I can't even begin to describe what this trip has meant, to my heart, to my soul. To have seen and experienced all of this with you— there are no words."

"Oh, Gran. I'm not disappointed at all. I know exactly what you mean. After all of the majestic beauty we have seen, Las Vegas just does not seem the proper end for this trip."

"Yes, we can save that for another time."

"Yes, we will. Why don't you start getting things together while I take care of getting a flight booked?"

By early afternoon, all had been arranged and they were headed home. Both noticed the smiling attendant looking at them as they sat leaning shoulder to shoulder and their hands clasped.

"With the setting of the sun, dreams were shattered, one by one....."

I harbored thoughts of looking for other music—I know some of it exists by now. I never made that quest. I could not bear hearing his voice and not being able to reach out and touch his face.

I rose slowly from my chair, in no hurry to finish, but then walked deliberately to each candle in turn and extinguished its flame. Then I bowed my head to pray for Alain Philidor—for peace and relief from the pain that was approaching him all too quickly.

CHAPTER *30*

EUDORA WAS RESTLESS. SHE WAS not in pain and there were no no-
ticeable symptoms unless lethargy counted and at her age it probably didn't.
Sitting in the garden letting the slanting rays of sun touch her skin, she could
imagine that she felt the warm breezes of *Provence.*

Years ago, she had contemplated a trip there. And if she went to the
farmhouse? It would be in the run-down condition in which he had found
it. What would she do? Would she wander through the rooms remembering
this picture or that lamp? Would she look at floors and remember clicking
sounds of the heels of his boots as he strode across the stones or the sudden
muffling of sound as he stepped onto one of the rugs? Would she see the
beauty of what was to be or only dilapidated reality?

She pondered all of these things and in the end, knew there would be
no trip. She had not regretted the decision. It had been an idyll, a dream,
a reality that was all too brief, and now her chapter was drawing to its
end. Ironic that she would suffer the same finality as her husband. His, of
course, had been sudden, no warning, no hint that his heart would all but
explode in his chest. She thought hers would be a little more subtle. John,
who had been her doctor and friend for years, had been concerned and
prescribed medication.

She had become one of his first patients when he moved to town and
started a family practice. Many of the town's citizens were skeptical when

old Doc Avery had sold his practice to a Yankee, but John Randolph had won the respect of the natives with his quiet confidence, practice of sound medicine, and his deference to their customs and traditions. He never married so became the darling of every hostess and the extra man who could be counted on to be charming to whatever maiden aunt, sister, or cousin needed a dinner partner.

As a shadow crossed John's face, she knew that her condition had worsened. She reached out and gently took hold of his hand which still held the stethoscope to her chest. "It's not good news, is it?" She knew the question was rhetorical, but he needed a starting place for what he was to tell her.

Lowering the instrument, he took her hand in his. "No, it isn't." He looked directly into her eyes. "The deterioration has progressed much more rapidly than expected. I will increase your medication and that should make you more comfortable, but as we discussed after all of the tests and consultations with the specialists, there are no other options. I am so sorry." The last words were choked from a throat constricted by emotions long held back. "Eudora, I ...."

"I know, John." She patted his hand and reached to kiss his cheek. This was her friend more than doctor at this point. "Thank you."

"MISS EUDORA, MISS EUDORA." SHE could hear the words, spoken gently, then with a little more urgency. What was it this time, food, or medication? The voice was awfully persistent. Neither one was going to make a difference at this point. It wasn't that she had given up—just accepted. She had made use of the recent days recounting her life. It had been a good one. Joel seemed only a bad dream—far in the past—a child's nightmare.

Two relationships that could have been just never had the proper time to materialize. Herbert Tyler had been her lawyer since the death of her first husband. Only a few years older, he had shown a definite interest after allowing her a reasonable period of mourning. He could not know that Eudora's mourning went so much deeper and in a different direction—an unresolved mourning that consumed her. There eventually had been a few dinners, but Herbert realized the futility of pursuing any relationship other than professional. Eudora had been careful to not jeopardize that by giving any indication that she knew he would have preferred more.

John Randolph had been a different story. Eudora had been aware of his growing feelings for her, but it was too late. Alain and Cameron. They often merged now—the love of her youth and the love of her life. Together they had given her everything—they had also taken everything. She had nothing left to give except friendship. She was thankful for John, for his friendship and the professional care he gave her. She was comforted by his presence.

In recalling life's unfolding, Cameron filled the most space. The husband who had shared everything. He had given her Maggie, their beautiful daughter, loaned to them for such a brief time but who had graced every second with pride and happiness. Dory, who filled all but the loneliest corners. She had spent hours at her grandmother's side. They shared memories and love. She had just left the room to go pick some of the roses that Eudora had whispered a wish for.

Somewhere, just at the edge of recognition there was a shimmer—a memory taking shape. A face with sculpted cheekbones, flowing hair and almond eyes that still glowed with passion. *Alain.* Raging against fate that had given him to her, only to snatch him away, had been stilled. In the ensuing quietness he lived—the beauty of him, the gift of him.

"Miss Eudora." This time the words were tinged with panic and accompanied by a tentative shaking of her arm.

"Gran," the roses dropped to the floor and Dory dropped to her knees beside the bed.

Eudora, did not—*could* not—take time to reply. She was walking through a meadow filled with flowers, as familiar as though she had been there only a moment ago.

Cruel time did no more in preparing us to be torn apart than it had our entering each other's lives. It gave us moments and then left us to live with the consequences.

CHAPTER *31*

DORY SAT IN STUNNED SILENCE. The letter dropped from her fingers onto the table. She closed her eyes. The past several days had been a blur—burying Gran, beginning to sort legal and business matters. Now this! The lawyer had told her that everything was set up in a trust—everything in order. Between her parents' and grandparents' estates, she was quite a wealthy young woman. But this was something different entirely. It seemed an innocent package left for her by her grandmother, but it had sent her reeling.

This defied belief, denied coherent thinking.

First there was the letter addressed to her. As she began to read, her initial thought was that Gran had been delusional. No, Eudora had never exhibited any signs of dementia. Perhaps in the rest of the contents there would be some clue, some explanation.

There had to be.

But there were no answers, only more questions. There was a letter addressed to someone named Alain Philidor, in France. There were instructions regarding the letter. They only added to her confusion. There was a very thick, well-worn journal.

Perhaps it held answers.

Dory opened the book. There was an entry written on the inside cover.

In the month of June, 1952, I left the sticky summer heat of Booneville, Mississippi and embarked on the great adventure of flying to France to spend time in Provence. That in itself was an unheard-of expedition for a Southern lady, but that was not the most unique thing about the holiday. Circumstances spiraled beyond bizarre when I met Alain Philidor while trespassing onto his land in order to find the perfect spot to dab my paints onto canvas.

I knew from the beginning that he was a special man, and the farmhouse he had so lovingly restored to a special place, but I did not learn until too late that time was different in that place.

In the world I came from, calendars gave the year of our Lord as 1952—the calendar on the pantry door of Alain's cottage proclaimed that it was 2006! I had not intended to run that far...

Minutes ticked away before Dory could shift her eyes to the first page of the journal. The knot in her stomach tightened. The page was dated June 10, 1952.

I cannot find the words to speak of my first contact with Alain Philidor. Words. I cannot even find thoughts. All was revealed so slowly—the peacefulness of the place to sit and paint—the strength of the walls of the village I chose as my subject—the perfection of the day—the man sitting stoically watching.

The disappointment at not finding him in the meadow—the music of the stream calling to me—the beauty of him standing there, waiting—was he aware that he was waiting?

I did not accept his offer of dinner at his home—that was for another day—I knew there must be another day. I would not think of the implications of that.

In retrospect it should seem odd that we shared our deepest hurts during such an early meeting—it does not seem odd now, nor did it in that moment. It was as natural as a Sunday afternoon conversation between old friends.

A tap at the door of the conference room where she had settled to look at the package brought her back to reality. Literally, literal reality. She did not realize that she had been reading for over an hour. After the shocking beginning she had skimmed through many pages, then let her mind absorb the last few entries. Her world and what she thought she knew about it had been turned on its ear.

"Come in," she found her voice.

Herbert Tyler poked his head into the room. "Are you all right, Miss Walker? Is there anything I can get for you?"

A slight shake of her head. "Thank you, I'm fine." The expression became neutral. "Did my grandmother tell you what was in this package?" Had she shared this incredible story with anyone else?

"She simply told me that it contained her journal and some requests for you. My instruction was to give it to you, and I was to open it only if you were unavailable to do so. Are there any legal ramifications that need my attention?"

"Thank you, no." Dory began gathering her things. Tucking the book and letters into her purse, she stood and extended her hand. "Mr. Tyler, I appreciate the way you have handled Gran's affairs, and I am confident that you will continue to manage any legal matters connected with the estate. Thank you."

"Of course. It will be a pleasure to continue to handle the estate for you. I'll have an agreement drawn up for you within the week."

"Thank you." She left the office, the letters and journal a heavy burden in her purse.

———————

DORY DID NOT REMEMBER THE drive home. It was one of those so familiar—one where you find yourself at your destination without the slightest memory of the trip there.

The house felt empty. The housekeeper had finished her tidying for the day so was nowhere to be seen. Dory knew there would be food for lunch in the refrigerator, but had no appetite. She went upstairs to her room—the room that had been hers for as long as she could remember. After changing into casual clothes, she sat in a chair and surveyed her space—the setting for a young lady. The colors were now soothing neutrals accented by bright pillows and art that stated that the occupant had a flair for the dramatic.

Letting her gaze circumnavigate the surroundings, Dory remembered the ballerinas and pink walls from childhood. Then Gran had let her choose the bright colors and wild posters during her teenage years. She smiled, thinking of the sigh of relief Gran had emitted when she announced that she was ready for the current transformation. They had planned and shopped together.

Tears slid through the smile. "Gran, what will I do without you?"

And now this—she looked at the worn leather book lying on her bedside table.

She was Eudora's granddaughter. She would cope. No, more than cope. She began to plan.

At that moment in time you were there—healing my heart and touching my soul.

CHAPTER 32

WITH MONEY BEING READILY AVAILABLE, Dory was able to implement her plan at once. The first order of business was a trip to a music store. She purchased the music CD, *Four Point O*. The music was beautiful, especially the crystal-clear voice of the French tenor, Alain Philidor. The enclosed folder showed a handsome man with a look of mystery. A short biography included revealed that he lived in France on a restored estate. He was obviously quite accomplished as he spoke four languages, was a master on the piano, could acquit himself well on three other instruments, and was an amateur horticulturist. Dory stared at the picture, studying each feature. She read and listened and learned more about the group.

Aldo Agosto from Italy, also a tenor, had a softer more romantic voice. His dark curls and eyes were sure to capture the hearts of women around the world. He owned a vineyard in Italy and was interested in producing his own wines.

Representing the United States was Aaron Graham, the final tenor. With his blonde hair and piercing blue eyes, he looked like the boy next door. His passion had always been music. His parents had worked extra jobs to afford lessons for him. Now based in New York City, he provided scholarships for underprivileged students who showed musical promise.

Antonio Ferra was Portuguese. He, too, was endowed with the Latin good looks. He was the baritone of the group, providing a rich, resonating anchor for the melodic voices of the tenors. He did not share the agrarian interests of his European band-mates, but lived in Lisbon in a modern apartment which housed his art collection.

The internet provided a treasure trove of information about the group. Singing "crossover" music explained why the group did not receive a lot of airplay. They simply didn't fit into the restricted genres of radio stations. Still, Dory was surprised that she had never heard of them. Their voices were beautiful, and they seemed to have quite a following in Europe and Japan, with a growing audience in the USA.

She wondered if her grandmother had ever been tempted to buy the music or go to a concert. A concert, of course. That needed to be the next step. Once again, the internet provided the needed information. The group was just finishing an extended tour by playing limited dates in the United States. Their final concert was to be in Atlanta the coming weekend.

Evidently the group was more well-known that she realized because the best seat Dory was able to get was well back in the auditorium. She would have chosen a seat well away from the stage anyway as it certainly wouldn't do to have him look into the audience and think he was seeing Gran. For the first time in her life, Dory felt a bit unsettled by her striking resemblance to the young Eudora, though she had heard it remarked upon all of her life.

THE CONCERT HALL WAS ELECTRIC. The audience, much of it comprised of mature women, was abuzz with anticipation. The group took the stage to loud cheers. As she listened to the music and watched Alain Philidor, so many of Eudora's words swam in her head. Even when he was not singing, her eyes could not leave him. She tried to visualize her grandmother as a young woman with him. She could not make a connection. Time, once again bewildered, confused, and perplexed a woman at its mercy.

THEIR TOUR WAS OVER, AND the band fell out of the public spotlight. Dory did no further research or information gathering. She had no explanation for her lack of movement to continue with her loosely knit plan for carrying out her grandmother's instructions.

Indecision can only be tolerated for a short period of time. Dory had finished an early light supper and started for the veranda with a glass of wine when she wheeled abruptly and walked to the music center where she put in the CD. Taking her wine, she left the door open so that the music drifted outside. The voices caressed, curled around her, sat on her shoulder, and whispered in her ear.

The wine glass shattered when it hit the flagstones. It had slipped from her fingers as the face of a handsome tenor swam before her when his lilting voice performed a solo part.

She needed to move forward—sitting, letting strange fantasies evolve would not be productive or healthy.

———————

HAVING CONVINCED A PRIVATE INVESTIGATOR that she was indeed not a lunatic stalker, but a woman who was willing to pay handsomely for his services, it took him only a short time to provide the requisite information. She may have hinted at writing an article for a prestigious magazine, but she was pretty sure it was the prestigious amount of cash in the envelope she had placed on his desk that brought her the information that Alain Philidor was at his home in France.

———————

SHE HAD BEEN A GUEST at the Hotel Gounod for three days and explored the immediate area around the fine old building. Two hours were spent in the Church of St. Martin, meditating, and reading passages from the journal. Just as Eudora had found peace and answers in the solitude of the ancient church, so did Dory. She would simply have to see if the gentleman was at home. Just showing up at his door might not be the most polite of introductions, but what could have been said in a phone call? Most likely he would have dismissed her as a fan, and any chance of seeing him would have been lost.

Guided by descriptions in the journal, Dory was sure she would be able to find her destination. Armed with the book and accompanying letters, along with strong resolve and curiosity, she set off into the countryside.

ALAIN PHILIDOR STOPPED ABRUPTLY AND stared in disbelief. A face, his face, stared out at him from the window of the antique shop. "What?" Inside and looking over the backdrop in the window, he knew at once that it had to be the portrait that Eudora had been painting of him, but how did it come to be in this shop? The clerk could only tell him that it had been bought by the owner after it was located a few days ago in an old storeroom at the Hotel Gounod. The manager who sold it had mentioned that it looked to have been in storage for quite some time, probably abandoned by some guest. This added further to his state of utter confusion. He paid the asking price and waited in silence as the purchase was wrapped in brown paper and handed to him.

The drive home was a blur, his mind whirling. The old pain, the old joys, were relived. The new questions had no answers.

There was an unfamiliar car, a rental, in the driveway.

"Alain, I am so glad you're here." Anna came hurrying in from the kitchen.

"There's a strange car in the drive." He was on guard. The group had become well enough known that there had been some instances of fans trying to gain access to their personal lives.

"A woman just arrived. When I told her that you weren't here, she said she would wait for you. She just walked in and then went straight through the kitchen and out into the garden—like she knew where she was going. I was just getting ready to call you when I heard you pull up. Do you want me to call the police?"

Alain hesitated. "No, I'll see what she wants." He laid the package on the table in front of the sofa then walked to the kitchen door. There was a woman by the old table. She was looking out across the open fields.

When the door opened, she turned. He staggered backward.

Alain's face registered disbelief, his vice wavered, "You're…."

"A relative," Dory quickly interjected. "Mr. Philidor, my name is Dory Walker, and I've been asked to deliver a letter to you." She held out the sealed envelope. She let out her held breath when he accepted the letter with a skeptical look.

He indicated for her to sit, then dropped onto one of the chairs opposite her. He scrutinized her face—there were definite differences, but she looked so much like Eudora. Perhaps he was imagining the similarities. Maybe he didn't really remember Eudora so clearly, heaven knows he had tried hard enough to erase her from his mind.

He looked at the letter. "Who sent you?"

"I think it will be much easier if you just read the letter before we talk."

He shot her a wary look but opened the envelope, unfolded the single sheet inside and began to read.

My Beloved Alain,

Please read the journal that accompanies this letter. I hope that it is being delivered in person but if received by post, please suspend disbelief of the impossible and believe what it says. You will know from details included that it is true.

The hurt I must have caused you has been a deep sadness for me. Believe me, my darling, it was not of my choosing to leave. My one desire was to stay and spend my life with you. I have cherished the memory of every second we spent together, and those memories have sustained me. I have taken comfort in the knowledge that it is not too late for you to have a full and happy life.

Always in my heart,
Eudora

He jumped to his feet, "What kind of sick joke is this? I don't know what kind of scam you are running, but you need to get out of here." He stood looking down at the woman who made no move to get up. Where had this letter come from? Who was she? How did she have this information? How had she found him?

"Mr. Philidor, please. I know this is a shock, but if you will just look at this journal, particularly pages I have put markers on, I think that will tell you enough that I can begin to explain some things."

He stood looking down at her. She didn't seem to pose a threat. The idea that she was a stalking fan was dismissed. The letter was certainly a shock—was it truly from Eudora? He sat and reached for the book she extended to him.

In the letter, Eudora had asked that he suspend disbelief in the impossible—that was what would be required to believe what was written here. From time to time, he would look up at the woman with a questioning expression, but she just indicated he should continue reading. Suddenly he froze again. He was looking at the page with the drawing Eudora had done from memory. His eyes quickly scanned the entry.

I was blessed to have been able to draw Alain just as I remembered him from that day. In memorializing his face, I have done all of which I am capable to never forget my time with him—never forget that we loved.

But it is time to move on. It was an interlude, and I have accepted that in my head, and my heart will gradually adjust. Interludes in our lives can be brief or extended. They can be chosen or forced upon us. They can be times of serene happiness or fraught with anguish. But they are interludes, a 'time out' that, while affecting our lives, are not the continuum in which we live. They can be quickly forgotten or indelibly stamped into our reality. They can bring resolution and peace, provide respite but no answers, or introduce new elements that carry their own dilemmas. But they are interludes, never to be repeated. If fate is kind, we are given someone special with whom to share that time.

My time in France was an interlude and fate was kind—I shared that time with Alain Philidor.

The look he turned toward Dory was one of confusion and frustration. "Please, come with me." He led the way into the living room and indicated for her to sit on the sofa. He placed the journal open to the picture Eudora had drawn on the table in front of her. Reaching for the package, he removed the wrapper and laid the painting beside the open book.

"Where did you find that?" Her shock was evident in her voice.

"I purchased it just this morning in a shop in the village." The painting and the picture in the journal were almost identical. Dawning reality was the beginning of acceptance—still, his brows were knitted, and he slowly shook his head from side to side. "I do not believe this. How can this be?" His logical mind could not allow for such a possibility.

"I don't know. May I read the final passage to you?" She picked up the book before he answered.

Alain Philidor was not out of place. He belongs in that lovely old farmhouse that he has restored—in the proper time. His time is now. This is what cannot be explained, but I do know that it is true. He was from this time in my future, and he loved me. And I loved him.

Dory closed the book and turned to face an incredulous Alain. "Who are you?" He suspected what the answer might be.

"I am Eudora Imogene Walker. Eudora Winningham was my grandmother." She spoke quietly, gently.

He could only shake his head and repeat, "How...?"

"I don't know, Alain. I don't know how this happened. Gran often talked about love and its lack of limitations. She would sound very mysterious and once, when I tried to question her further as to what she meant, her eyes became misty, with a far-away look and she said, 'Love knows no time or space.'

I thought she was just thinking about Granddad and missing him. Now I'm pretty sure it was you she was thinking about."

He reeled as one drunk. She was *real*, and she had loved him. She had come across time to touch his life, or perhaps she had come across time so that he could save hers. He had no doubt that if she had stayed with her husband, he would have eventually hurt or killed her.

As, one by one, facts he had read and heard began to take root in his consciousness, he suddenly leaped up and bolted up the stairs. In seconds, he appeared at the top of the staircase and slowly descended. His face was utterly expressionless. Deliberately, he unfolded the fingers of his closed hand over the table holding the journal. Eudora's ring dropped onto the book.

He looked at Dory, who sat in stunned silence.

"I don't understand. I searched for her. I could not find a clue that she was ever here. I tried, by telephone, to find her in the town of Booneville, Mississippi. There was no trace to be found. I do not understand." In such a short period of time, much had been explained, but so much remained unknown.

"Wait, let me find a certain entry." Dory picked up the journal again. She found the page she was looking for, looked up into his bewildered eyes, and began reading.

I have spent days, weeks, trying to answer the question, how? I know now that is not just a single question. There are smaller questions within it. I have thought about how I did not notice differences and thought anything that did catch my notice was due to different location and culture. I realize now that in his presence, I was not always vividly aware of my surroundings. I am convinced now that it was very likely that the time was different only when I was with Alain, perhaps only in his cottage. I will concern myself no further with the details of how.

She ceased reading and closed the book.

Slowly, a calm came over Alain. He had not been delusional. It had all been real. The diary, of course, would have to be locked away—it would only be tabloid fodder and likely provoke mockery. He looked at Dory—so like her grandmother. Eudora looked out at him through her eyes. He must not linger on thoughts along this line, must not fall into the trap of thinking she was his Eudora. That Eudora had been a reality that didn't exist. Yet, for those summer days, she had existed. He could still feel her in his arms and still smell her scent of jasmine perfume.

But it was time to let go.

"Shall we go sit in the garden with something cold to drink?"

His invitation surprised her. "I would like that very much."

She picked up the journal and followed him into the kitchen.

He prepared tall glasses of lemonade himself as Anna was not in evidence. It would take a good deal of thought as to the explanation she would be given. He smiled, realizing that at the thought of explaining Dory's presence, he was assuming that she would be here long enough to make that necessary. He led the way back out to the table under the oak.

The ease with which they conversed proved to Dory his total acceptance. At first the conversation was filled with questions. What had Eudora's life been like? What had his life been after she was gone? Gradually, there was a subtle change. Questions about how he restored the cottage, the village, the surrounding area....

"I would love to see those horses...." She broke off, but need not have worried about what he would think of the bold statement.

Alain paused only a second before asking, "May I take you tomorrow to see if we might catch sight of them?"

She looked directly into his eyes. "I would like that."

He gave her a mischievous look and after a short pause asked, "Do you have a silver pattern?"

"Chantilly."

An invisible thread connects those who are destined to meet, regardless of time, place, or circumstance. The thread may stretch or tangle, but it will never break. —Ancient Chinese Proverb

WANITA MARIE HUMPHREY LIVES IN Jefferson City, Missouri, with her husband, Glen. She enjoys spending time with her family and friends, writing, traveling, and going to concerts.

While teaching for thirty-one years in Missouri's Public Schools, Wanita was active in the Missouri State Teachers Association and served as state president in 1999. She is a member of Kappa Kappa Iota and PEO, a philanthropic organization dedicated to awarding scholarships to women.

What are some of the most interesting things Wanita has done? She was the first girl to take Coaching of Baseball at Missouri University. She also has a trophy for winning a late-model stock car race and has visited all fifty states. What is something that she would like to do? Go ziplining!

Find out more about Wanita and her writing at
www.wanitahumphrey.com

www.ingramcontent.com/pod-product-compliance
Lightning Source LLC
Chambersburg PA
CBHW031000260626
47169CB00002B/623

* 9 7 8 1 6 3 3 7 3 6 9 8 6 *